The P...
STRANGER

The PERFECT

The PERFECT STRANGER

ALISON KENT

BRAVA

KENSINGTON PUBLISHING CORP.
http://www.kensingtonbooks.com

BRAVA BOOKS are published by

Kensington Publishing Corp.
850 Third Avenue
New York, NY 10022

All Kensington titles, imprints and distributed lines are available at special quantity discounts for bulk purchases for sales promotion, premiums, fund-raising, educational or institutional use.

Special book excerpts or customized printings can also be created to fit specific needs. For details, write or phone the office of the Kensington Special Sales Manager: Kensington Publishing Corp., 850 Third Avenue, New York, NY 10022. Attn. Special Sales Department. Phone: 1-800-221-2647.

Brava and the B logo Reg. U.S. Pat. & TM Off.

ISBN-13: 978-0-7582-1115-6
ISBN-10: 0-7582-1115-5

First Kensington Trade Paperback Printing: April 2007
10 9 8 7 6 5 4 3 2 1

Printed in the United States of America

To Theresa Weir for Amazon Lily.

Chapter 1

Tequila and Mickey Finn.

A hell of a bachelor party guest list.

A jackhammer morning-after headache.

José Cuervo might be a sumbitch, but the bottle didn't deserve the blame for the hangover that had J. Jackson Briggs pressing the heels of his palms to his eye sockets.

His spinning head was all about waking on a cold, concrete prison floor, an AK-47 five inches from his nose jump-starting his day with a jolt.

The stumbling trip he'd taken at gunpoint—from his cell, down a dark corridor, into a military command center—had terrorized him into nausea.

And now here he was, stuck holding his tongue because he wasn't so backwater that he didn't know not to piss off his host country.

He didn't care that the charity-based Smithson Engineering crew had just signed on for another back-breaking, year-long stint in the jungles of San Torisco.

He didn't care that the contentious nature of the military dictatorship characterized a nation on the brink of total disaster.

He didn't care that he was the construction site's only chopper pilot. He was ready to go home. To the States. As soon as he was outta here, he was outta here.

And it couldn't happen soon enough to suit.

Irritation spilled down his back along with his body's physical response to San Torisco's tropical climate. Ninety-eight percent humidity and a new sheen of sweat drenched his work shirt.

He didn't want to know what had dried in his hair, matting it in a crust to his skull. He didn't want to know what constituted the brown stains on his green fatigues.

He especially didn't want to consider when or how his boot laces had been chewed through.

All he wanted was out.

The coat of puke green paint slapped across the floor in *El Comandante's* headquarters did little for his mood or his stomach.

Rocked back on two legs of a rickety chair, he eyed the machine gun five feet away on top of the scarred and battered metal desk. The additional distance gave the weapon a new perspective, one no less menacing.

From here, however, he could see the eyes of the uniformed man behind it. They were as cold as the floor he had slept on, as black as the darkness summoning him down.

He refused to look at the woman sitting in the chair three feet from his side.

Twisting the tight gold band around his left ring finger, Jack released a sigh, then burped up a blast of the chemical churning in his gut.

The burn up his throat told him there'd been more in his glass than the shot of tequila he'd sloshed there sometime before midnight.

Then, his buddy Brad's bachelor party had been in full swing, and Jack had been lucid, sober, and still the wedding party's best man.

Six hours later he'd come awake to find himself a prisoner.

And the groom.

He wondered who'd slipped him the Mickey, who'd added the wife.

Most of all he wondered why.

"Once more, *Señor* Briggs. And this time be warned that my patience grows thin."

Comandante Mosquera pushed the parchment document across the piece of furniture that was a scratch-and-dent reject, then sat back and swiveled his chair side to side. "Is this, or is this not, your signature?"

Jack brought his own chair down hard and snatched up the paper. Elbows on his knees, he forced himself not to sway to the maddening *squeak-squeal, squeak-squeal* of the other man's seat for fear he'd tumble to the floor.

Instead, he focused one bleary eye on the *Partida de Matrimonio.* Certificate of marriage. The real McCoy. One hundred percent. Eighteen karat. Sure as sh—

"*Señor* Briggs!"

"Yeah, it's mine," Jack bit off. With a flick of his wrist, he spun the parchment back onto the desk. No one did that backward left-handed scrawl like J. Jackson Briggs. He'd recognize it in a heartbeat.

"*Bueno. Muy bueno.*" *Comandante* Mosquera dried his forehead in the crook of an elbow, the sweat stain one more service medal decorating his olive-drab uniform. Adjusting his beret over his slick black hair, he tapped his desk with a length of bamboo cane.

A sharpened length of cane, Jack ruefully noticed.

"You . . . you . . . *Americanos.*" *El Comandante* spit out the word with great disgust, gesturing in the air with the crude weapon. "You come to our island. You treat our homeland like you treat your own. Selfishly, you take what you want. Never do you give thought to the burdens you will leave behind when you go."

"Look." Jack raised his palms in a gesture of false concession. "You've got the wrong guy. I'm not going anywhere or leaving anything behind. I'm here to do a job at the request of the Sabastiano government. *Your* government.

"In fact," Jack said, on a roll, "your dictator, Carlos Sabastiano himself, is picking up the tab. The way I figure, you owe me—"

Whack!

Bamboo cane hit metal desk and snapped. Three inches of pointed stick landed at Jack's feet. He glanced up.

The lethal-looking blade now protruding from the hollow rod wasn't crude at all, and only slightly more intimidating than the malevolence in the other man's eyes.

Comandante Mosquera spiked the blade into the desktop's wooden surface. The cane quivered with the backlash. Jack swallowed hard.

"Why you are here does not concern me, *Señor* Briggs. What you do while you are here you will answer for."

"Look. Sir," Jack forced himself to add, when the commander's nostrils flared. "All I'm doing here is working on the road the Smithson crew is cutting from *Ciudad* Torisco into the mountains."

The Latino's eyes narrowed dangerously. He eased to his feet, skirted the desk, stopped directly in front of Jack's chair. With his feet planted shoulder width apart, the commander made an intimidating tower.

"You deny that you American men find our San Toriscan women to your liking?" Mosquera asked, smoothing down his thick mustache with forefinger and thumb.

At the change in conversational direction, Jack hooked his thumbs in the belt loops of his fatigues and leaned back. "The scenery's been great, yeah. Why do you ask?"

A keening sob rose into the air, a sound so awful Jack wondered whose grave he'd stepped on. Before he could so much as turn toward the screeching woman—his screeching *wife*— the AK-47 gouged the bridge of his nose.

He gagged back the bile shooting up his throat, closed his streaming eyes, and tried to pray.

Now I lay me down to sleep . . .

"Your wife seems to find your little . . . what do we say . . . disregard for the situation most inappropriate."

Jack licked his dry lips and managed to croak out, "What situation are we talking about here?"

El Comandante answered with a growl and a sharp twist of the gun barrel.

Searing heat shot to the top of Jack's head. He bit his tongue; the metallic tang of fresh blood seeped into his mouth. His face beat like a tom-tom, burning hotter with each pulse of blood.

And then, just like that, the pressure vanished.

Jack pitched forward. He caught himself before hitting the floor, then blinked, blinked again, and sneezed.

He wiped his nose with the back of his hand, then dried it on his pants, leaving behind equal parts mucus and blood as he focused a furious gaze on the man across the room.

Comandante Mosquera sat on the edge of his desk. The gun dangled from his fingers like an extension of his arm. "In our country, *Señor* Briggs, when a man takes pleasure with a woman he is no longer a free man."

He picked up the marriage certificate and studied Jack's scrawl. "Our women are taught their obligations from the day they are born. They are instructed by their own mothers to care for their future mate. To provide him children. To provide him a home. To provide him loyalty and service.

"In doing so, they honor our ancestors. They know nothing of the choices your American women have." *El Comandante* ended his lecture with a snort.

Jack gingerly tested the split skin on the bridge of his nose. "Yeah, well, it's not called the land of the free for nothing."

He heard a tiny snuffle at his side, then a chuckle—no, a

cough. Knowing he could avoid the bad news no longer, he peered between two fingers to get a good look at his *wife*.

From the look of things, he'd bagged himself a winner.

Worn brown fabric, drab and inclusive, enveloped the woman, from the top of her head, down her shapeless form, to the pink toenails at the end of ragged rope sandals.

A tendril of dark hair peeked from beneath the head covering, giving him a clue that she was—

Wait a minute. Wait just the hell a minute. Pink toenails? *Pink toenails?* Uh-uh. No way was he sitting still for this scam.

Jack pushed to his feet. "Whatever's going on here isn't going any further until I talk to someone from the American Embassy."

"*Señor* Briggs. I am not taking orders here." *El Comandante* raised his gun-toting arm. "You, on the other hand, will do exactly as I say. Unless you wish to face the consequences."

He released the safety, flexed his trigger finger, and sighted Jack's throat. The barrel loomed closer.

Tasting gunpowder and metal and his own mortality, Jack considered his options for the length of time it took the other man to pick up the blade-bearing cane with his free hand.

"What is it I'm supposed to do?" Jack asked.

"First, you will sit down."

Jack was slow to respond, slow enough in fact that he caught a brief flare of indecision in the other man's eyes before the cold blackness returned.

Good. He'd made his point. The chair he sat in might be unstable, but he wasn't.

Comandante Mosquera arched one thick brow, then gave a brief nod of approval. "*Muy bueno.* Now, *Señor* Briggs. Your wife is in need of your escort. She must journey to her family home in a mountain village."

Jack straightened. The chair swayed. "I'm the only chopper pilot Smithson's crew has. We're laying fifteen hundred feet—"

El Comandante brandished the cane point and cut off Jack's sentence. "Once you are there, your wife and her family will make the final decision on whether or not you will be a worthy husband. Because of this questionable course of events, if she wishes an annulment she will be granted one."

Jack perked up. A quick trip up the road might not be a bad idea. Especially if he came back a free man.

He pretended to ponder *El Comandante's* proposition when, in truth, he wondered why the San Toriscan military was meddling in personal matters.

How much backup did this guy have? Or was he an elite member of the Sabastiano private *Policía*, answering to no one but the big man himself?

Jack swore succinctly, but silently. Everything about this deal stank of hidden agendas. "I don't have any say in the matter?"

"You have a say in nothing."

His palms pressed to his thighs, Jack stood, wincing at the dizzying rush of blood that swept through his skull to the center of his face. "Then let's go."

One corner of Mosquera's mustache lifted. "*Señor* Briggs. What is your hurry?"

"I'm under deadline. Hank Smithson doesn't have time to waste looking for me."

"Do not worry. We will inform your . . . how is it you say . . . your foreman at the Smithson compound where you will be for the next month."

Jack needed a shovel to pick up his jaw. "The next month?"

"Of course, *Señor* Briggs." A sneer greased the Latino's lips. "You cannot return until the baby is born."

The baby? *The baby?*

Jack's heartbeat signaled a situational slip from bad to worse. He whooshed in a serious breath and slanted a glance to the side . . . and his *wife.*

"What baby?"

She stood then, his burlap sack, and turned his way. Jack

never saw her face. He never got past her figure. Past her belly that had to be at least eight months gone.

He remembered well the changes that developed between seven and nine months. He'd measured Mandy's waistline every week until Justin had been born.

But that was forever ago. In a limbo sort of time and space he'd tried to forget.

All he knew right now was that playing handball didn't make a baby, and that was as close to getting any as he'd come the last year.

Stunned, Jack sat. His butt cracked hard against the wooden chair. The legs cracked out from beneath him. His head cracked against a piece of standing concrete block.

And the last image that lingered as he fell to the ground was *Comandante* Mosquera's smug crack of a smile.

Chapter 2

Jack woke the first time to the pitch and sway of a chopper going down. He lunged forward in a panic, wildly searching for the stick to level the craft.

His groping hands found nothing but air, nothing to save him from the crash to come, nothing but wide-open fields below and the still, silent air that amplified screams until he could hear nothing else.

Not even his own thoughts. Not even his heartbeat. Not even the prop above chopping the air like a scythe.

He scrambled and reached, struggled to control the diving craft. There. He had it. The stick. No. A bone. Covered with blood. Tagged with warm flesh.

Jack screamed.

Chapter 3

Jack woke the second time to blessed peace. He waited for the angels, listened for the harps. Finally, he sniffed, expecting the smoke of fire and brimstone.

All he smelled was himself. The stench brought him awake. That, and the donkey bray that split the air.

The roaring bellow might've been music to a horse's ears, but it boosted Jack's headache into overdrive.

The headache revived the pain in the center of his face. The pain brought the word "puke" to mind, along with the realization that he was no longer in jail.

When he finally pried open the one eye that wasn't swollen shut above his aching nose, he saw nothing but knothole. So far, so good.

A few seconds and a deep breath later he rolled onto his back, tucking his chin to his chest.

He was in a peasant's donkey cart, no doubt the property of his *wife*.

Six bags of beans shored up one side, while the other owed its forty-five-degree angle to a railroad spike wedged against the rotting floor.

Oh, yeah. He could hardly wait to see the place she called home.

He eased up onto his elbows, continuing to sniff. The air was dank and damp with tropical stagnation. The kind of air that was truly hard to breathe.

The raucous racket of jungle birds resounded through the trees. A flutter of red and yellow wings beat against fronds tangled in swaying vines.

Pieces of blue sky dotted the thick growth miles above his head. Extra-large insects buzzed and droned, looking for a square of human flesh.

Jack figured he was safe. At this point his smell would scare off the septic man.

"Hey," he called out. Surely his wife hadn't deserted him so soon. He needed to know exactly how far from civilization he was.

A spit bath was out of the question. He needed a shower. A river. A puddle. He was long past proud.

"Hey!" He shifted higher, jarred to a half-sitting stop, and groaned. The vine hanging overhead had a head of its own—and was headed his way.

An eyelash viper. Right up there at the top of Smithson's list of *Things to Avoid While Working in San Torisco*. Not that he'd needed the warning.

The snakebite he'd suffered during a stint in Burma had turned him into a true ophidiophobe.

"Yo. *Señora* Briggs." She had to be out there somewhere. And if she didn't show up in about half a second, she was going to be a widow.

He hadn't moved a muscle other than those it had taken for the gruffly whispered call, but that tiny movement seemed enough for the snake.

The head arced around. The beady eyes gleamed black. The tiny tongue flickered.

Damn, but Jack wished he could remember how to pray.

The snake slithered closer, hovering mid-air, dangling by the tiniest bit of coiled tail.

Crack!

The whip stung Jack's left ear, snapped the snake from the tree. It fell to the cart: head over the rickety side, tail in Jack's lap.

The top half reared up. Jack jumped, fell back, hit his head on the railroad spike, and watched the downward arc of an eighteen-inch blade.

The machete severed the snake in two. The head thunked to the ground. The tail writhed in his lap.

Jack gladly let tequila and fear take him down.

Chapter 4

The third time Jack woke he smacked his lips and tasted Tequila Mickey, the stubborn demon who'd taken up residence in his gut. The parked cart was still in one piece, and a shuddering glance revealed no viper parts left behind.

Neither was there any sign of *Señora* Briggs.

A quick physical inventory assured him his nose only felt like it was broken. The swelling had receded. The gash had begun to heal. The rest of his parts seemed to be in working order—some working overtime.

He needed to pee like a racehorse.

Fully upright for the first time since those lovely minutes in *Comandante* Mosquera's office this morning, or yesterday morning, or the morning of the day before, Jack took a minute to do nothing but absorb his surroundings.

The muted beams of fractured sunlight. The thick growth that hinted at the rutted trail behind. The brackish smell of the tropics, and the sounds.

The job site rumbled daily with shouting men, dynamite and tumbling rocks, sledgehammer on steel, but none of those noises compared to the echoes in the trees.

Twitters and caws and the brush of wings on leaves. The

croak of frogs, the chirp of insects, and water. Gurgling. Lapping. Green and ripe.

Jack scooted to the end of the cart, pushed himself off, and managed to stand. Barefoot. He looked down, frowned, and wiggled his toes in the crushed undergrowth.

He had no idea where he was. He was a man without a mission, a weapon, or a clue. He didn't even have a pair of boots or a change of clothes.

The only thing he knew for certain was that he was not the father of that baby. He would not have forgotten having sex. But that damned marriage certificate . . .

Drug-induced duress. Surely that would work as grounds for an annulment if her family gave him any grief.

He didn't do drugs well, so he didn't do them at all. Even alcohol was a gamble. The half inch of tequila he'd downed the night of Brad Buckley's bachelor party had seeped into his veins like straight bourbon. Anything chemical on top and *poof*!

Whoever shanghaied him from *Cantina Mañana* must've been mighty pissed to end up stuck with an incoherent idiot. Served the suckers right. He just wished he knew who they were—and what they wanted.

But some things wouldn't wait while he searched for the pieces of the puzzle. So he took a step to the corner of the cart, reached for his zipper, and arced a yellow stream onto a stunted fern.

Hugely relieved, he gave the plant a Vulcan salute. "One-hundred proof, son. Live long and prosper."

Now about that water.

Scowling, he considered his bare feet, flexed his toes, and shrugged. If the natives could do it, he'd give it the ol' Boy Scout try.

He headed into the brush. The prospect of a body that smelled more of man than beast made it easier to ignore the wet stuff squishing between his toes.

Vines clutched his arms and neck. Branches lashed and whipped his bare head, pulling at the roots of his needed-a-haircut hair.

Insects swarmed thicker here, going for his eyes, flying up his nose, even dive-bombing his feet. Jack slapped at his upper arm, smashing a palmful with one blow.

Bugs he could deal with. He just hoped the decapitated viper hadn't left any vengeful relatives hanging around.

And that whoever had saved his ass with the Indiana Jones whip-and-knife routine wasn't in the mood for human target practice.

Grimacing at the reminder that he wasn't alone out here—wherever the hell *here* was—he turned at the sound of a splash.

Visible now through the thinning undergrowth, the water beckoned. He pushed his way through a tangle of vegetation and found himself at the edge of a steep embankment.

He glanced briefly at the vines hanging from the mangrove trees that grew at the water's edge, then ignored any self-delusion that he was Tarzan, sat, and slid on his backside down the slope.

He had one leg ankle-deep in the water when a twig cracked behind him.

"I would not do that if I were you."

It was the first time he'd heard her speak.

Her voice was so soft he did well to make out her words. All subtleties such as accent and emotion escaped him, even when he thought to mentally double-check.

He turned to the side. Her shadowy form loomed at the edge of the ridge above. Leaving his foot exactly where it was, he took a deep breath.

"I don't know who you are. But you're not me. And I'm not going another mile until I have a bath."

"Then look to the other bank."

He squinted across the width of water, wishing for the know-how and time to turn that rugged hide into a pair of boots so he could stomp back up the incline and explain to his *wife* that he was on one side, the croc on the other, and a good bit of water swirled between.

Instead, he bent to cuff up his other pant leg and took a defiant step into the river. "I'll be out of the water before he even thinks to dive."

"He will not dive."

"Look." Abandoning what patience he still had, Jack gestured expansively. "I know I smell more like day-old than fresh—"

"It is not the smell. It is the piranhas."

Though he'd done his best to convince the Smithson crew otherwise, Jack really didn't have a death wish. Still, he refused to move except to strip off his shirt.

The shallow water was clear enough that he counted the pebbles on the bottom. He intended to take whatever bath he could, and if a man-eating fish wanted to take him on, he was damn well in the mood.

With one eye trained at river level, he squatted and sloshed water under his arms and over his chest, lower jaw, and neck. While carefully bathing the skin around his nose, he scanned the bank in both directions.

The Smithson barracks sat on the delta of the Rio Verde where the river met the Caribbean Sea. He'd flown over enough of the construction area to have a good grasp of the island's layout.

But this was new. Strange. Nothing, dammit. Nothing. Not even a tree that looked familiar.

He stood and reached for his shirt, water sluicing down his torso to soak the waistband of his fatigues. Gingerly, he dried his face, then shrugged back into the khaki.

Abandoning his search for landmarks, he clambered up the slippery rise and crashed through the underbrush after the one person who could answer his questions.

When he reached the clearing, he stopped three feet from

where his wife crouched before a tiny fire. She didn't seem the least bit concerned that he'd managed to make it back in one piece.

Fine. This was as good a time as any for a marital heart-to-heart. "Do you mind telling me where we are?"

She made no reply. Instead, kneeling on the opposite side of the small flame, she leaned forward and blew against a stick of kindling.

Jack couldn't see her eyes. Her hood concealed the upper half of her face. Elegant fingers held the covering against her cheeks.

Her lips were soft, not chapped. Her skin barely tanned and smooth. Her cheekbones were high. Her nose narrow and long.

The picture voided his preconceptions about the mountain people. A mishmash of Latino, Indian, and mulatto heritage, the natives lived in squalor at best. The women were aged at twenty.

So how old was his wife? Sixteen? Twelve?

Curiously wary, he reined in his temper. The kindling caught, and she lumbered to her feet. Head bowed, she tucked her hands up in her loose-fitting sleeves.

Jack gestured toward the flame. "Is this your idea of home cooking?"

Her lips curved upward in the briefest smile before she ducked her head and walked to the front of the cart. After digging through a canvas bag under the seat, she returned with a flat pan and a rolled banana leaf.

Squatting at Jack's feet, she punched up the fire.

From the leaf she withdrew a golf-ball-sized lump of damp meal, patted it between her hands, and slapped the flattened cake onto the pan.

Jack's stomach flip-flopped at the smell of hot corn.

She cooked side one, flipped the cake over, and fried side two, the pan jiggling over the fire like Jiffy Pop®. A slave to his stomach, Jack could only salivate, and when she tossed the cake in the air, he was ready.

He shuffled the food hand to hand, blowing on his fingers until hunger won out. By the time the first bite had burned a path to his stomach, he was chewing on his second. With number three, he hit his stride.

With one bite left, he noticed that his wife hadn't eaten. In fact, she'd all but packed up the evidence of their stop. Everything but the fire.

He frowned. "You're not going to fix yourself something to eat?"

"There is no time." She finished stowing her gear in the cart and, by the time she returned to the fire, the single square inch of food in Jack's hand weighed what felt like a pound.

He offered her his last piece. "You want this?"

She shook her head. "You eat it."

He felt as if he hadn't eaten for days, so he shrugged and popped it in his mouth. "Are we making camp here?"

She added more fuel to the fire. The flame flared up, producing no smell and only a wisp of smoke. "No. We must be on the road before dark."

"How far is it to your family's village?"

"It is not far. A day or two into the mountains. But if we do not pass the Sabastiano *Policía* outpost by sundown, we will be delayed another day."

"*Policía* outpost, huh?" Jack wasn't sure whether his heart picked up in fear or loathing. "Why don't we wait until after dark? From what I've seen, Sabastiano's private guards aren't too keen on Americans working in their country, papers or not." He turned his pant pockets inside out. "I'm paper poor at the moment."

"We have our marriage certificate," she answered, dusting her hands together.

"Right. That." As if he needed the reminder.

"But not to be alarmed. You will not be passing through as an American laborer."

He took a step forward. "You want to run that one by me again?"

She pursed her lips into a thoughtful bow. "You will be disguised."

"As what?" As crusty as it was, his dirty blond hair didn't come close to the native black. And at six three, he had a good half foot on all the local men he'd seen. This was going to have to be some kind of disguise.

"First we must get rid of your American clothes." She nodded toward his fatigues and unbuttoned work shirt, her gaze lingering long enough on the damp patches of his bare skin to make Jack tense.

He wouldn't miss this particular uniform that was a whole lot worse for wear. But still . . . "I guess you have my new wardrobe stashed up your sleeve?"

She smiled again, that totally discomfiting curve of lip. "Yes, I have other clothes for you, though they are not, as you say, up my sleeve."

"Figure of speech." Jack shrugged out of his shirt.

Head bowed, she stepped close and took it from his hand. The backs of her fingers grazed his chest, briefly lingering, and then she moved away.

He damned himself for noticing, but he'd been right. Her hand was soft, smooth, coolly sleek, and he wondered about the rest of her skin.

Hesitantly, he shucked off his pants, shoving them at her before changing his mind. But he drew the line at his boxers. He was near enough to naked to prove embarrassing if she decided to strand him.

"I need your underthings, too."

Jack scowled at her bowed head. "Why?"

"The pants I have for you are very thin and the top only as long as your hip."

"So?"

She gestured toward his shorts. "Those red lips on your

underwear will be visible through the cloth. Such is not normal wear for a San Toriscan."

"They nail me for an *Americano*, you mean."

"Yes. They do."

Great. Just great. He shook his head. "So, you gonna give me the clothes?"

"Once you give me the shorts."

"Uh-uh. No way am I standing here bare-assed in front of you and that donkey."

She shrugged, took a step back, and dropped his fatigues on the fire.

Jack lunged forward in a panic. The unexpected heat sent him back. The cloth disintegrated in seconds, leaving but a spoonful of ashes.

What the hell was she using for fuel?

"Hey, I could've washed those."

"We must not have them with us in case of a search."

He didn't like it that she made sense. "I guess you plan to burn my drawers, too?"

"*Sí.*"

"Fine." He made a "gimme" motion with his hand. "The clothes."

She lifted the hem of her skirt. Scuffed-up toes of heavy black boots peeked from beneath her ragged black underskirt. She raised the burlap higher. Then higher.

No way was he wearing a dress. "Wait just a minute here."

But by the time she had the skirt rucked up to her waist, wearing a dress was the least of Jack's worries. Remembering how to breathe topped the list.

Reaching back, she unhooked her "baby," tossed him the canvas knapsack she'd had tied around her waist, and dropped the top skirt back to her ankles.

"You're not pregnant." The dress hung blade-straight to the ground, not an inch of rounded belly between shoulders and knees. Jack couldn't even think to move.

"Your shorts." She held out one hand.

"Uh-uh. You drag me into the jungle, posing as a pregnant woman, no, a pregnant *wife* needing my help, and you want me to give you my drawers? I don't think so. In fact, I'm outta here." Jack started walking.

"You've been in the back of the cart three days, *Señor* Briggs."

Jack stopped walking.

"We followed a road that leaves no trail. I'm the only one who knows where you are, the only one who knows how to get you safely out of here. You give me the shorts or we both may very well die."

She'd walked toward him as she talked. A step for every two or three words. She stood close enough that all he had to do was reach up and push the hood off her head to see her whole face.

The machete tip inches from his nose dissuaded him.

One day, lady. One day, Jack thought, stomping to the far side of the cart where he shimmied out of his shorts. She caught them when he tossed, and Jack grimaced as they went up in flames.

He unrolled the canvas knapsack, shook out the paper-thin tunic and trousers, and draped both over the edge of the cart. They looked as bad as his fatigues. Butt naked, he stifled his complaints and dressed.

The fit of the shirt left much to be desired. The frayed sleeves barely hung to his elbows. And she'd been right about the length. The hem only hit his waist.

He struggled into the pants; the legs ended a good six inches above his ankles. The flax chafed every part of his skin that wasn't already raw and made him wish for a pair of tighty whities.

Hands out in surrender, he walked around the end of the cart and headed toward the fire. "You've got me. I'm who-knows-how-many miles from who knows where. These clothes would scare away a scarecrow. And even if I were to try and walk out of here, I'd no doubt lose my toes to jungle rot.

"Don't you think it's about time you let me in on the conspiracy? It's not like I'm the father of your *baby*. In fact, I'm beginning to wonder whether or not I'm even your husband."

Heedless of her blade, Jack grabbed her wrist and drew her close. "How about it, *Señora* Briggs? Married or not?"

"Yes, I'm married." Eyes burning bright, she jerked away and lifted the machete.

The tip of the blade caught the tie at her throat and nicked open the ragged neckline. Grabbing the material on both sides, she jerked and pulled.

The hooded dress fell to her feet. She kicked the pile of cloth away, then bent to scoop it up.

Dropping the burlap squarely on the flames, she defiantly faced him down, covered head to toe in a black habit and veil.

"But not to you."

Chapter 5

Jesus H. Christ! He was married to a pregnant nun.

Wrong, Jack. You're not married, and she's not pregnant.

But she was a nun.

She was also china-doll exquisite, a testosterone fantasy that sucker-punched Jack in his near-empty gut.

This woman had drugged him, kidnapped him, taken ten years off his life with the wife-and-child routine, burned his clothes, refused him a bath, and he still wanted to see her naked.

She was centerfold material, as close to perfect as a female got. Except for the tiny scar that bisected the arch of her right brow. And now that he looked closer, he wasn't too sure about her eyes.

It wasn't the exotic almond slant, or even the seductive get-me-drunk-Jack-Daniels gold. No. It was the way she'd seen a lifetime of too much, the way she saw too much now. Those eyes scared him.

No soft-voiced china doll should be so tough, so world-weary, or so wise. She was all three. She was a nun. And she was as Caucasian as he was.

Ignoring the machete she wielded like a sharp tongue, Jack glared down. "So, *Sister Señora Briggs*. Guess the marriage certificate was a fake."

She glared back, the fire in her eyes a one-hundred-proof whiskey burn. "Yes. But it was necessary."

"As necessary as that phony dialect of yours?"

Her chin came up, her shoulders went back. Defensiveness could have been her middle name. "I do not understand."

"You're as *Americano* as I am, *Sister*. And you've got the pink toenails to prove it."

Arms crossed over his chest, Jack leaned against the cart, watching as a change came over her slowly, a step off of denial and onto a soapbox.

The hand she had wrapped around the machete handle grew white, as white as the anger rising like a cloud of steam around her. "You're wrong, Mr. Briggs. I'll never be as *Americano* as you."

Why had he ever thought her voice soft? Even pitched low and minus the accent, the tone was as hard as the remains of the dynamited rocks he choppered out of the mountains.

And, dammit, why was his focus so blurred?

Her eyes, her voice, the ringlets of coffee-colored hair escaping her veil, none of that mattered. Except in relation to getting him home.

Jack swore on a sigh. "But I was right. You *are* an American."

"Only on paper," she replied, and when he cocked a brow she added, "My birth certificate. Place of birth. Boston, Mass."

Stirring up the ashes with the tip of the machete blade, she looked at him down her blue-blooded nose. Jack didn't care for the snub.

He might not have been long-term military material, but red, white, and blue still ran in his veins. "You've been down here so long you've taken on the San Toriscan causes as your own, huh?"

"The San Toriscan causes are my own."

He gestured toward her habit. "Yours and God's?"

"Mr. Briggs. I would suggest you do not ridicule what you do not understand."

Jack pushed off the creaky cart. "Oh, I understand enough, Sister. And I'd love nothing more than to be back in the good ol' U.S. of A. right now and see you get hard time for kidnapping."

She stomped on the remains of the fire, obliterating even the ashes. Then she stomped past him to the front of the cart, giving no clue that she'd heard his ultimatum.

Of course, he hadn't really given her one.

Yet.

"What I'd suggest, Sister *Señora*, is that if you want to get this show on the road you start talking with your mouth instead of with that blade," he added as she laid the machete on the seat to rummage in the burlap bag beneath. "We both know you're not going to use it on me. Now, I can come along peacefully or I can be a real pain in the ass—"

The whip stung the air milliseconds before it snaked around Jack's ankles. His head popped back. He went down hard. Flat on his back like Charlie friggin' Brown. His air whooshed out on a grunt. He strangled it back in on a groan.

Twigs and rocks dug into his backside. Damp leaves plastered themselves to his shoulders and head. Stars swam behind his lids, so he opened his eyes and watched the machete's downward arc.

"You, Mr. Briggs, are already a pain in the ass."

Her knee on his sternum made breathing impossible. She leaned over him, all haughty and regal, her skin heat-flushed ivory silk, her tendrils of damp hair dark in contrast.

His spirit more than willing, his flesh way past weak, Jack found himself seduced by her mouth—and the possibilities involved in their respective positions. But he'd always preferred to be on top.

So he shoved one knee between her legs, flipped her over, and pinned her to the ground.

Her wrists were tiny and porcelain smooth beneath his hands, her body pliant, soft, a memory of flesh-on-flesh and pleasure. He'd denied himself too long.

He lowered his head, his gaze fixed on her mouth. Her lips quivered and Jack caught back a groan. His gut clenched, contracted, knotted into a ball; he checked the urge to take things slow and met her gaze.

Her gold-brown eyes widened, first in fear and innocence, then shame and want. The flashing contradictions brought the picture into focus. He was about to make it with a nun.

A nun, for chrissakes!

Jack eased away, rocked back on his heels. She scrambled to her feet, dusted off her clothes, then grabbed up the whip and machete and scurried past.

Pulling himself together and giving her time to do the same, he tested his throat with two fingers, glad to find the moisture there to be sweat and not blood.

Glancing around, he worked to ease the ache from his ribs, rubbed the whip sting from his ankles, and watched the good sister drag a branch across what was left of that amazing little fire.

Fine. If she wanted to pretend like they hadn't lit a fuse of their own, okay by him. Back to business. Or at least to the present.

"How'd you do that fire thing? You know, no smell, no smoke. Spontaneous combustion of my clothes."

She recoiled the whip, stowed it under the seat of the cart. "It's the San Toriscan way, Mr. Briggs. You are too *Americano* to understand."

"A fact I'm mighty proud of, too, Sister." Jack stood. A half dozen steps toward the front of the cart he stumbled, then swayed, grabbing a handful of donkey for balance.

"Another of our San Toriscan ways, Mr. Briggs. Never let an *Americano* gain the upper hand." She gestured toward the back of the cart. "I'd suggest you get in while you still have the ability to do so."

Jack couldn't find the words to argue. The jumble in his

head that was the remainder of his mind swirled and sputtered behind his eyes. He staggered down the length of the cart.

Splinters pierced his sweating palms as he struggled to stay upright. He jammed his knee and nicked a hole in the skin above his kneecap in his first attempt to climb in.

The good sister gave him a leg up, then stood back as he landed face-first in a bag of beans. He squirmed his body around until his feet dangled off the end of the cart.

"Don't tell me. The corn cake." He spit out the words through the wad of cotton his mouth had become.

"I'm afraid I spiked it." Neither her smile nor her tone was the least bit penitent.

"That's why you wouldn't eat."

"I take my role as designated driver seriously, Mr. Briggs."

He should never have let her up. "I won't sleep forever, Sister. And you can bet your holy boots, I'll be waking up on the wrong side of the bed."

She propped her fists at her waist. "You seem so certain, Mr. Briggs. Perhaps you won't wake up at all."

Jack curled in on himself. His vision blurred into two nuns, then three. "Oh, I'll wake up. You need me, remember? Otherwise you wouldn't have held onto that pregnant peasant costume until I couldn't do a thing about it."

"You couldn't do a thing about it anyway, Mr. Briggs."

"Don't count on it, Sister," he mumbled, though he figured she was right. A whole convent stood in front of him now. "So, this is my traveling disguise? A drunk American?"

"Certainly not, Mr. Briggs." She leaned forward, pressed a cross and a rosary into his hands, and fastened a clerical collar around his neck. "You'll be traveling as a priest."

Chapter 6

Stirring to consciousness in the back of the cart, Jack experienced an eerie sense of déjà vu all over again. Then he shook his head and came fully awake, and determined to stay that way.

Nothing else was passing his lips unless he killed, cleaned, and cooked it himself.

At least this time when he belched he tasted corn and not any kind of synthetic drug. She'd used a natural sedative. More of those San Toriscan ways, no doubt.

San Toriscan or American. It didn't make a difference.

The world had sunk to a new low when you couldn't trust a nun.

Jack had to admit he'd had little contact with religious types during his thirty-nine years. His oldest memory was of the base chaplain, who'd directed a sort of all-denominational service every Sunday.

He'd been the same one who'd come to the house after the crash, the one who'd told Jack's mother that her husband had flown all the way to heaven.

Then there'd been the Air Force chaplain who'd sided with Jack's grandfather and tried to talk him into a lifetime of service rather than the four years he'd served.

The chaplain at the university had conducted Sunday after-noon services for the premed students who woke up in time to feel guilty about how they'd spent Saturday night.

The chaplain at the hospital had counseled the members of the aeromedical helicopter crew when the stress of flying and fighting to save lives got to be too much.

But the closest Jack had come to a nun had to be Julie Andrews in *The Sound of Music*. Julie'd been a doll, a syrupy sweet stick of candy.

Jack's nun was a chili pepper. Spicy. Hot. Mouth-watering temptation. Her eyes should've belonged to an angel but were too old and damaged to be anything but human. Jack won-dered at the tragedies she'd seen.

Pushing aside the thought that came too close to sympa-thetic, he stretched every inch of his body and scrunched up his healing nose.

Dusk had fallen, the sky deep indigo and endless. Full of stars. And free of trees. While he'd been off in la-la land, they'd left the dense cover of jungle and stopped.

As thoroughly as the thick canopy of growth had prevented Jack from telling one compass direction from another, it had also done a good job camouflaging this traveling salvation show. Now they were free and easy prey.

The wide-open spaces had never seemed so wide.

He blinked, the click of his lids as loud as a shot in the night, held his breath, and listened. Nothing. Then the twitch of the donkey's tail. And a murmur of voices. Muffled. Spanish. One female.

The nun. No doubt pulling another scam.

He could barely make out a flicker of artificial light shining over the side of the cart. If she'd stuck to their itinerary, this stop should be the Sabastiano outpost.

And that would make the scam victims members of the Sabastiano *Policía*.

He opened his ears, closed his eyes, and prepared to do the

best priest routine he could manage—even though he knew most San Toriscans didn't put a lot of stock in Catholicism.

The island of San Torisco sat between Venezuela and Haiti and was steeped in the latter's vodoun beliefs. The population itself was a mix of the South American mestizos and the mulattoes of the Caribbean isles.

The divergent mix of ancestral beliefs left a lot to interpretation, including their bastardized forms of religious worship. And one thing Jack had learned, if he'd learned anything at all, was that Carlos Sabastiano was the biggest bastard around.

Within a ten-mile radius of *Ciudad* Torisco, prosperity abounded; the natives in the valley proclaimed Carlos Manuel Sabastiano heaven-sent. Hell lay in the mountains, where the most basic amenities were nonexistent.

Accessibility to the clinics in the valley pretty much depended on the villagers' creative minds. The transportation of choice seemed to be *tap-taps*—pickup trucks converted into rickety buses—or donkeys, solo or hitched to a two-wheeled cart. The way down was rough and rocky, the way up the same.

When Carlos Sabastiano had opened his coffers and agreed to pay for the construction of a road into the mountains, the U.S. contingent of the World Relief Team had been ready.

They'd called in Smithson Engineering, knowing Hank Smithson for the good ol' boy philanthropist he was.

The multimillionaire got his kicks by challenging corporate America to match his humanitarian projects dollar for dollar. Not that he needed help subsidizing his ventures; he could've built a stairway to heaven on his own.

The man just happened to have a heart bigger than his wallet and couldn't understand why he suffered the affliction alone.

His crew knew that and enjoyed having their work scrutinized by the older man's eagle eye, because when Hank Smithson said "Good job," the praise was sincere. When he asked his men's opinions, he wanted honest input.

When he added that bonus to the payroll envelopes on December 31, every man on every crew counted his lucky stars and found Hank Smithson the brightest.

That was why Jack had hesitated voicing his opinion on this particular job. Even bigger than Hank's heart was his belief in human nature.

And everything Jack had seen in the last twelve months led him to believe that Carlos Sabastiano, the San Toriscan dictator, hadn't undertaken this project for the good of the people at all.

If Hank found out after the fact that he'd financed a project to be used for criminal gain, it might just take the fight out of the old man.

And if, unlike Jack, Brad Buckley had survived his bachelor party and still planned to retire to the tropics with his sweet young wife, Jack could hardly ignore his duty to warn his friend—and he would, if he ever saw him again.

As if on cue, the murmur of voices grew louder. Obviously the good sister didn't need her whip and her machete to make a point.

Jack might've pitied the poor recipient of her razor-sharp tongue if his life hadn't depended on whatever story she was telling.

After all, she *had* used the word "die."

He strained to make out the words. His Spanish was good enough to grab the gist of a conversation, and since he wasn't going to get a dress rehearsal, he wanted to be as prepared as possible for his role.

A door off to his right creaked open and a rectangle of dim, yellow light spilled across the cart.

"I'm sorry, Sister. Travel beyond this point in the valley is not permitted after sunset. Under no circumstances can I allow you to go on."

The guard's voice never quavered, a feat Jack admired coming from a boy who sounded like he hadn't yet learned to shave.

The sister exhaled a long-suffering and motherly sigh. "I am sorry as well, but I must insist you let us through."

"It is for your own safety, Sister," an older voice—though not by many years—added. "The darkness holds many unforeseen dangers."

"But we must go now. And God travels with us." The sister's voice rose in intensity but not in volume. "The Mass cannot be delayed any longer. What with the heat, and the preparations for the *Festival de los Santos*, the body cannot remain unburied another day."

A hesitation. A quiet discussion. A shuffling of feet. Jack sensed the guards' uncertainty. The mention of heat and dead bodies had him more than a little queasy himself.

Then the conversation grew heated, decidedly negative, and the Spanish too rapid to follow. Jack fingered the rosary, stopped, then slid the beads through his fingers again and tested the weight of the silver cross in his palm.

A heavy dose of Catholicism upside these goons' heads might be their only way out.

He rolled up onto his knees. The cart shook beneath him. With a step and a misstep he gained his feet, reeled to one side, and teetered back.

The corn cake tied a rebellious knot in his stomach, and he couldn't find his balance. His hands felt like lumps of clay as he fumbled with his weapon.

The beads tangled on the cross, the tinkle of jet on silver ringing like music in the night. Jack wrenched them apart; arcs of light shot off the silver crucifix. His arms fell to his sides like dead weight.

Whatever the sister had slipped him had the nerves from his brain to his limbs on strike.

He squinted against the frame of light shining from the

thatched hut. Machine guns slung over their shoulders, two guards flanked the doorway. His nun stood between the men, facing them down with bravado and justice and God on her side.

Sister *Señora* turned. The Spanish discussion faltered, then stopped, both guards wide-eyed and wider-jawed.

And as young as Jack had hoped.

"*Houngan.*" The uniformed baby face nearest the guard shack pointed Jack's way.

"*Damballah!*" The other guard gave his own opinion.

They both stepped back, whether awed or frightened Jack didn't know. He upped the ante.

He might not know his Hail Marys, but he could conjure enough Latin to give these guys a good scare.

"*E pluribus unum. Semper fidelis. E pluribus unum. Quid pro quo. E pluribus unum. Semper fidelis. E pluribus unum. Quid pro quo.*"

He strung the words together in a monotonic chant. It did the trick. The donkey lurched forward. Jack wobbled, caught his foot on the beans, went down to his knees.

The good sister followed suit. She made the sign of the cross, steepled her fingers beneath her chin, and started to pray.

Jack could've sworn he heard her mumble, "Pain in the ass."

The guards panicked. One dropped to a kneeling position and mimicked the sister's motions. His comrade jerked him up by his uniform collar and dragged him down the road to open the gate. The chain-mesh barrier creaked on its frame.

With a rapid wave of their hands, the guards motioned the cart forward, tugging back the heavy gate an inch at a time to make room.

"Let's go, Sister," Jack muttered.

She crossed herself again and rose. Not bothering to dust off her knees, she approached the cart with all the subtlety of a fire-breathing dragon.

"Mr. Briggs. Don't you dare move another muscle or open your mouth until I say so." Gripping the side of the cart, she leaned toward him, her face scant inches away.

Jack closed half the distance between them. "Get me out of here and your every wish is my command."

"My only wish is for you to shut up."

"You don't want a love slave for the rest of your life?"

"You will not live that long."

"And here I thought we'd be telling our grandchildren about this adventure."

She rolled her eyes, and by the low lamplight spilling from the hut Jack saw the golden glitter. The urge to touch her overwhelmed him, and his hand was halfway to her face before he had the good sense to withdraw.

Leaning his back against the seat of the cart, he curled his fingers into a bag of beans instead. "It's too bad you're a sister, Sister."

"What makes you say that, Mr. Briggs?"

Their gazes met, held. The air between them sizzled and steamed. Filled with danger and primal heat, the thick jungle night stole Jack's breath. When he didn't answer right away, she dismissed him with a shrug and boosted herself up.

He touched her then, trapping her hand with the back of his head. A touch no one could deem inappropriate. It was harmless, simple, as totally platonic as a touch could get, but she didn't move.

In that small second, that sweet shot of time, more than their gazes clicked and collided. And he knew she knew he wasn't the one holding her there.

"Mr. Briggs?"

Jack cleared his throat. "I've changed my mind, Sister. It's a damn good thing you're a nun."

Chapter 7

The question of propriety came after that, after she'd climbed up onto the seat, clicked her tongue at the donkey, and jostled the cart through the gate.

After that Jack took a minute to think.

What had passed between them was nothing. Just a matter of timing and adrenaline. That need to confirm one's mortality in the face of certain death.

Wasn't sex one of the key factors to affirming life? If not, then what was all that mushy stuff between Bogart and Hepburn at the end of *The African Queen*?

He shook off the moment and looked up. The guards couldn't get the gate closed fast enough. And once they were back inside the hut, they doused the light—that tiny beacon that lit the way back into the valley.

The valley . . .

Wait a minute. Wait just the hell a minute. Jack scrambled up and over the seat and settled himself beside the good sister.

She slanted him a glance, then scooted maybe a whole inch toward her side of the bench. "Mr. Briggs, I'd prefer it if you stayed in the back of the cart."

"Oh, I'm sure you would." Hunched forward in the low-slung seat, Jack draped his arm across the one-by-four that served as the backrest. "Tell me, Sister. How come if I've been in the back of the cart for the three days that you say, we're just now leaving the valley?" He grabbed the reins away and jerked the donkey to a stop. "Why'd you lie to me?"

She afforded him a quick flick of her gaze to his face before returning her attention to the crude road winding like a ribbon into the dark mountains beyond. "I told you the truth. You've been in the back of the cart for three days. I did not say we had been traveling."

Son of a bitch. Jack eyed her squarely. "I'd call that a sin of omission, Sister. And don't think your American blood or your phony pious attitude will make a difference in a court of law."

When she continued to stare straight ahead, Jack dragged his palm down his three-day stubble. She'd fooled him again, damn the woman. For all he knew their little campsite had been within walking distance of the Smithson barracks—even if he hadn't recognized the place.

At that thought, another dawned, and Jack frowned. "How long was I in jail?"

"Only overnight." She took the reins from his grasp and slapped the donkey's rump. "And if you don't let us get on our way, you'll be spending many more nights there. We are still too close to the outpost for safety."

Jack was through taking every word she spoke as law. "I don't see those two as the hot-pursuit type. They couldn't wait to get rid of us."

"What it won't take them long to realize, Mr. Briggs, is that they were fooled by a trick of light. What they saw was all an illusion."

"You were standing next to them, Sister. Tell me what they saw." He glanced over and waited for her answer.

She took a minute to form her words, her lips pursing. "The silver cross reflected the light thrown from the hut. With the way you were weaving on your feet, the light appeared to travel in an arc."

"Like jerking a flashlight back and forth?"

She considered his description, her frown drawing attention to the scar above her eye. Jack wondered how she'd got it— and if it had anything to do with her machete.

"Similar," she finally said. "But not as bright. Plus you undulated and swayed like a snake, like you had no bones or spine."

He had felt pretty spineless, but he still didn't understand. "So?"

"When a vodoun worshipper is possessed by a loa, a vodoun spirit, he takes on the characteristics of the loa riding him. Damballah is a rada loa, the father of all that is powerful and good. His signature is the serpent."

"You seem to know an awful lot about voodoo for a Catholic." He made the statement casually, but could tell she took it to heart.

Her face grew blank. She laid the reins across her lap; a sheet of ice went up between them. "I know more than anyone should ever be forced to know."

He didn't know if she was speaking to him or to herself, but he did wonder if the word "forced" had caused the drop in temperature. He let the subject go. For now.

"So, the guards thought I was possessed by this Damballah. Interesting," he said, voicing his thoughts, then asking, "What was the other thing they called me?"

"Houngan. An initiated priest of vodoun."

"They're getting their religions a mite confused."

"Roman Catholicism is the official faith of San Torisco," she said, reining the donkey around a cart-sized rut. "But vodoun offers the natives solace in their present lives and the anticipation of a better life in the hereafter.

"A San Toriscan's life is hard, Mr. Briggs. Vodoun lessens the misery by giving the people a way to contact the spirit world. It's a truly joyous experience," she said, adding snidely, "Of course, you won't find ceremonies conducted in the valley."

"Why's that?"

"Carlos Sabastiano has proclaimed vodoun the backbone of San Torisco's poverty and ignorance."

"Let me guess. Carlos wouldn't be too thrilled to find his *Policía* boys practicing what he preaches against."

Her lips drew into a tight, thin line, then twisted up in a bitter smile. "Carlos will go to any lengths to enforce his beliefs, Mr. Briggs."

So he'd been right. Carlos Sabastiano wasn't the saint he made himself out to be. Jack started to ask more but the good sister cut him off.

"Overall, your performance was an eerie combination. The light. The tinkle of the beads. You moved like a man possessed. That and your hissing Latin chant."

"I got us out of there, didn't I?"

Her shoulders lifted in a small shrug. And then she smiled. "*E pluribus unum?* It must have been quite a few years since your last Mass."

"You're looking at a good ol' Southern Baptist, Sister," he said with a laugh. "And I figure I did pretty good considering I never had time to squeeze in Latin 101 between Human Anatomy and Psychology."

"You're a doctor?"

"Nope. Four years of Air Force and three years of premed were all the structure I could deal with." The wheel on his side jostled over a bump in the road. Jack grimaced and leaned toward his left.

"And call me Jack. Mr. Briggs reminds me too much of my grandfather. But then, he'd be Colonel Briggs." Jack's laugh grew sharp. "Pretty funny, huh?"

"How so?"

"Mr. Military being named after a military jail? The brig? Damn hilarious. Of course, he didn't belong to the Corps. He was Air Force to the bone." Jack snorted. "The name fits either way. I grew up in his prison."

"You lived with your grandfather?"

"No. Just on the same base. My dad died when I was ten. After that, my grandfather felt it his patriotic duty to turn me into the man of the house."

"What happened to your father?"

"He was a test pilot, out there punching holes in the sky."

"And you became a pilot like him."

"Not like him. Never like him." And even as he said it, Jack knew it was a lie.

He, too, had chosen the sky. The challenges and barriers a daily game he thrived on. Instead of thriving on Mandy and Justin. Instead of keeping his feet on the ground. Instead of being the husband and father they needed.

He forced his mind back to the present. "How did you know I was a pilot?"

"You are here because you are a pilot."

"And why is that, Sister?"

"You'll find out soon enough, Mr. Briggs."

Damn this waiting. The minutes and the road passed by in silence. The moon lit the sky with a bluish-white light, enough to see the road vanish into the dark.

To the right and left, trees stood sentinel-tall, guarding the secrets behind them well. The steady plod of the donkey's hooves and the uneven sway of the cart were about to rock Jack to sleep.

He wondered how far they were going. He wondered where they were going.

Then he wondered how many lies she'd told.

"You want me to drive, Sister?"

"No thank you . . . Jack."

He smiled. "What's your name, Sister?"

She seemed to consider for a minute. "Jillian."

"Okay, Sister Jillian. I'm guessing here that the day or two you said it would take to get to your village is the same day or two I slept through," Jack surmised, wishing his head was one-hundred-percent straight.

This puzzle-wrapped-in-a-conundrum-wrapped-in-a-riddle business was for the birds. "Which means we're not dealing with a matter of distance here but a matter of time. I'm guessing, too, that we're not going to any village, considering no marriage and no baby means no annulment and no in-laws."

"Patience is a virtue. You'll find out all you need to know in a few more hours."

Hours now. Not days.

"The way I see it, Sister, I've been a fairly cooperative kidnappee. But we're sitting ducks here. Why don't we pull this donkey to the side and find cover until morning? I don't relish being ambushed in the middle of the night."

"We won't be."

"If a ranking member of the *Policía* swings by on patrol and finds out those two boys back there let us go, that machete and whip won't put a dent in an M-16."

"Oh, ye of little faith." She shook her head. "This part of the jungle has eyes, Jack. Friendly eyes. In the valley, we were on our own. Now we are not far from help should we need it."

He released an impatient sigh.

"I know you must be frustrated and I'm sorry, but I cannot say more."

Sorry didn't cut it in this case. He needed information. "Okay, your first objective was kidnapping a pilot, your second getting out of the valley." Jack numbered the goals on his fingers. "I guess the pregnancy routine comes into play here somewhere."

Sister Jillian guided the donkey to the right. "San Toriscans do not take intimacy lightly."

He toyed with the ring he still wore. "So, if I had shirked my duty and refused to marry you—"

She arched her scarred right brow. "If you had refused to marry the mother of your child, you would not have seen the light of day again."

Not that he was planning anything dumb or drastic when he was in the middle of only God-and-the-sister-knew-where, but . . . "What if I had abandoned ship back there when you were still carrying my baby—"

"I would have found another pilot."

"And brought Mosquera down on me?"

She shrugged.

"You'd have let me go to prison knowing I was innocent?"

"All causes require sacrifices. The nobler the cause, the greater the suffering."

Slumping back, Jack shook his head. Mosquera had told the Smithson crew he'd be gone for a month. That meant he was on his own. "Who helped you cook up this little scheme?"

"Please, Jack. Do not ask anything else. You will find out everything you need to know as soon as we stop."

"Fine. Okay. I'll shut up." And he did.

He even went so far as to crawl into the back of the cart, figuring he'd stretch out, catch a few uninterrupted z's.

He actually dozed for a while because the next thing he knew he was looking at a sky streaked with pinks and blues and enough foliage overhead to suggest they'd left the main road for a less traveled path.

In fact, as he listened to the creak of the wheels and the plop-plop of the donkey's hooves, he heard voices. A small encampment came into view as he looked on. Pitched tents sat in front of thatched huts, and a sizable fire burned in the center of the clearing like a community stove.

He smelled fresh, hot coffee and decided once they stopped he was going to stick close to Sister Jillian and eat whatever she ate.

The hell with cooking and cleaning it himself. He was starved.

Four women stood around the fire preparing what looked like a feast of a breakfast. He smelled onions and potatoes and chili peppers. And fresh hot tortillas.

The cart lurched to a stop; Jack scooted to the end, his legs halfway off when one of the women looked up and noticed the new arrivals.

"Gabriel!" she called toward the nearest tent.

The tent flap opened and a khaki-garbed man ducked through. When the woman pointed in Jack's direction, the man turned his gaze toward the cart.

His combat boots stirring up clouds of dust, he approached at a brisk stride, carrying an air of authority on his wide shoulders. He raked his longish hair off his forehead. It fell back around his face, framing a smug and disturbingly familiar smile.

Jack turned to question Sister Jillian, but she was already scrambling down from the seat of the cart.

He got to his feet, dread writhing in his stomach like a deadly eyelash viper gone rogue.

And the rest of his world tumbled.

He looked on, watching as Sister Jillian walked briskly toward the man called Gabriel, losing her habit on the way.

By the time she reached him, she was down to a black-ribbed tank top cinched in with a cartridge belt and fatigues tucked into military boots.

The machete bounced against her hip, and her hair, released from the veil, tumbled to her shoulders in a mass of unruly waves.

He'd been off on the color.

It wasn't coffee at all, but caramel.

And not only wasn't she pregnant, now she wasn't a nun.

Could he be any more screwed?

Laughing, a tinkle of triumph that echoed without mercy, she threw her arms around Gabriel's neck. Effortlessly, the

Latino lifted her, swung her around, then holding her suspended, stopped and stared over her shoulder directly at Jack.

Jack had seen those eyes before, and he swallowed hard.

Sister Jillian's Gabriel was none other than *Comandante* Mosquera in the flesh.

Chapter 8

"Glad to see you made it through in one piece," Gabriel said, the familiar timbre and warmth of his deep voice swirling through Jillian's exhaustion.

She needed this welcome home desperately. The stress of the last few days had nearly driven her insane. "Everything went as expected. What about you? Any problems?"

"Not a one," he said as she stepped from his arms, brushing several strands of hair from his face. "We got here earlier than anticipated. Esteban's men have a surveillance net surrounding the camp. Rosa has taken charge of the fire and the rest of the women—"

"As usual," Jillian interrupted to say.

Gabriel winked, then pointed off to the right. "Joshua is down at the creek with Angel Garza. The boys said they're tired of beans and potatoes so they're fishing for their own breakfast."

Jillian's heart picked up speed. "Is that safe?"

"C'mon, Jillian. Being careless wouldn't keep me alive."

"I know. I just—"

"Worry. I know. Now stop." Gabriel draped an arm over her shoulders and hugged. "Tell me about the trip up. Esteban kept you advised?"

She nodded, finding sanctuary synonymous with Gabriel's arms. He'd gotten her this far; he would see her through to the end. "We circled Verde Point until Esteban assured me the American search parties had abandoned the main roads. We camped last night at the Rio Verde clearing."

Smiling inwardly, Jillian recalled the look of abject terror on Jackson Briggs's face when he'd come eye-to-eye with that harmless tree snake.

He reminded her of the green kid she'd been when she'd come to San Torisco thirteen years ago, though she doubted he was half as idealistic.

Or anywhere near as naïve.

Even now, glancing around Gabriel's side, she watched a flurry of deep emotions—none of them nice—flash across Jack's face. The next instant his expression went blank, a casual mask hiding his thoughts. But his body was a coiled spring.

Jillian wondered if she'd have time to react to his pounce.

And whether she would want to.

"Jillian?" Gabriel prodded.

"I'm sorry, what?"

"You made it through the outpost without any problems?"

Problems? She wouldn't know where to begin. "We made it through fine. The priest getup made for a convincing argument."

"Good, good." Gabriel rubbed a thumb and forefinger over his clean-shaven upper lip. "Now, we wait for the WRT transport to show up at the point, and after that . . ." He shrugged.

"You think we can pull this off?"

"We can't afford not to."

Jillian rubbed at her temples. "You mean *I* can't afford not to."

Gabriel threaded his fingers through hers and pressed their joined hands to his chest. "We're in this together."

"To the bitter end?"

"I won't let it go that far."

His strength sustained her. The beating of his heart was an affirmation, an effortless statement that he'd be there for her always.

"Hey." With a tender swipe of his thumb, Gabriel dried the dampness from the corner of her right eye. "Why don't you introduce me to your priest?"

Jillian nodded, knowing she could avoid Jack no longer and feeling like scum for all the lies she had told.

Necessary lies, she reminded herself, hating the way she had employed the sort of self-serving machinations she abhorred. The same *do unto others what needs to be done* attitude that had caused her to break all ties with her family.

The only things she'd taken with her when she left home at eighteen were her five feet eight inches and one hundred fifteen pounds. Those, and the single-minded determination to right a wealth of wrongs.

Things hadn't changed in the last thirteen years. Except that she'd filled out to one twenty. Okay. One twenty-five. But she knew from the way Jack studied her face that he was seeing the chameleon act the rest of the Boston Endicotts pulled off with ease.

Even as young as nine or ten, she'd wondered how her father could stand up in Congress and plead the cause of human rights, then come home and walk past Marguerite and Marco, their San Toriscan housekeeper and her son, like they didn't exist.

Especially after the praise Congressman Endicott had received for rescuing the Chavero family from their poverty-stricken life here on this very island. Her father's hypocrisy had first puzzled, then sickened her.

Discovering the truth later had sickened her even more.

Though lives depended on the lies she now told, deception went against everything she believed in. What she'd spent the last half of her life fighting for. Honesty, integrity, morality.

All of which she'd abandoned when faced with disaster and her need for Jackson Briggs's skills.

She swallowed hard and followed Gabriel. His stride certain, her best friend approached the tall American who, with a simple glance, a teasing turn of phrase, had been the first man in a very long time to make her body ache.

Jack stood by the edge of the cart, those stupid pants halfway up to his knees, that ragged shirt so small his arms seemed to skim the ground, his bare feet and tousled hair the image of an overgrown kid.

But the look in his eyes was feral, savage, anything but innocent. He was a cornered animal, turned to face the hunter and ready to fight to the death.

She wondered how he would feel if he knew the real reason they'd had to get out of the valley last night. That she couldn't keep him drugged forever, that her cargo was too precious to have a dim-witted pilot at the controls.

That if he'd woken up lucid in the Rio Verde clearing he'd more than likely have heard the morning make-ready sounds of the men he worked with. They'd been that close.

Damn. When had this simple plan become so very complicated?

That one's easy, Jillian. You slipped the man a four-hour Mickey that took him three days to get over.

Well, how was I supposed to know he couldn't handle it?

C'mon, haven't you learned yet to expect the unexpected?

I know. I know. But forced flight at gunpoint would have been so much easier than all this deceit.

Yeah, but physical force doesn't make much of an impression on a man who's dead to the world.

Jillian screwed up her courage. She stepped around Gabriel in time to see Jack tense. Unsettled or not, he held his ground and Jillian chalked up another point in his favor.

Gabriel laughed. "It's okay, man. We really are the good guys."

"Somehow I'm having a hard time buying that."

Jack ignored Gabriel's proffered hand. Hitching at the thread-bare waistband that sagged on his lanky frame, he sized up the other man with a steady look.

Jillian recalled the sight of his bare shoulders and chest, his tight backside, his air of don't-try-to-put-one-over-on-me. She thought of the fire in his eyes. Of the way his body moved with a natural grace. The way he caused a stirring in her blood.

He was gorgeous, one hundred percent American male, and the kidnapping took him out of her reach. Lacing her fingers together, she turned her palms out, wishing the two of them could somehow start over. Wishing they'd met before events and time had driven her to this.

"You're not pregnant. We're not married." He jerked his thumb toward Gabriel. "He says he's one of the good guys. And now you're not even a nun. Is there anything about you that's real, Jillian?"

Yes, she had deceived him, but for a cause she deemed worthy. A cause she would give anything for, including her own life.

"Jack, please understand neither Gabriel nor I mean to hurt you. Once this mission is completed, you'll be released unharmed."

He stared at her as if she didn't exist. Fine. As long as Gabriel's planning worked out, she'd never see Jackson Briggs again after the end of the next week.

Pity, a renegade part of her thought.

But when the supply boat docked at the point and the *Policía* stepped in to intercept it, she and Gabriel would make their move, and after that, Jack would be gone.

Wondering what he'd be like in bed was a waste of time and energy best spent elsewhere.

Jack pulled her into focus, pride riding high on his shoulders. "Having an American citizen taken hostage doesn't sit too well with the U.S. government. And don't think Hank

Smithson won't check out whatever story you two fed him. You can bet your sweet corn cake he'll demand facts."

Jillian stuffed her hands in the pockets of her fatigues and lifted one shoulder to shrug off Jack's concerns. "I was hoping this would be one adventure you might share with your grandchildren, Jack."

The moment grew taut, tension thickening the air along with the day's rising heat, the incessant humidity, and Jillian's steamy thoughts. Jack's gaze grew bolder, brazen, arrogantly challenging, and sexually smug. She tried to look away and failed.

Miserably.

Of all the pilots and all the construction sites, why did he have to be the one working hers?

Finally, an inquiring brow lifted her way, Gabriel stepped forward. Jillian welcomed the reprieve, dispatching Gabriel's unspoken question with a subtle shake of her head.

She didn't know what Jack wanted.

She wasn't ready to find out.

Gabriel turned to Jack. "Sorry about the nose, Jack, but nothing's as convincing as reality. Jillian, you think you got something to put on that?"

"I'll get some salve from Rosa." Jillian turned to go.

"Wait just the hell a minute." Jack raised one hand and gripped the edge of the cart with the other. "This game has gone way beyond dress-up, and I don't think twenty questions will cover all I want to know."

Gabriel shook his head. "I'm afraid I'm not the answer man, Jack. But I'll do the best I can."

"You mean the best you will."

"In this case? One and the same."

Jillian looked from one man to the other. If she'd ever had a doubt Jack would do, the calculating look in his eyes dispelled it.

"I want to know who you are. Both of you."

"Gabriel Roberto Corteze. Born and raised in El Paso, Texas. MA in political science from UT El Paso, and eventually I'll finish my doctorate. Currently I'm Corps Leader for the World Relief Team in San Torisco."

Gabriel finished and gave Jillian the go-ahead. She took a steadying breath and said, "Jillian Paige Endicott. Born and reared in—"

"Boston, Mass." Jack cut in, then narrowed his eyes. "Endicott? As in Congressman Endicott? Ambassador to San Torisco?" Swinging around, Jack paced down the opposite side of the cart and back. "How goddamn convenient," he murmured to himself as he walked the same path twice, finally grabbing hold of the cart's slatted side until the whole thing shook with his suppressed tension. "If you needed a pilot so badly, why didn't you walk into Smithson's camp and ask?"

The heat of his angry gaze reached all the way to Jillian's toes. "Believe me. I tried. It was impossible. The Sabastiano *Policía* patrol the compound 24/7. Even if I'd been able to get in, it would have taken an act of Congress to get us out."

Jack shoved both hands through his hair, the look in his eyes truly wild. "In that case, why didn't you just call Daddy and get him to buy you a flyboy? Hell, why stop there? Get him to buy you your own chopper. You'd look real good in an Apache, Jillian. All those missiles and rockets." He laid a finger alongside his nose. "If you're gonna do a body damage, you might as well make it count."

Jillian's throat swelled until she could barely breathe. How dare he. How dare he!

"You think you know so much? Well, hotshot, for your information I haven't spoken to my father in ten years. My work here may seem to be in sync with his, but trust me when I say our goals are polar opposites."

"What exactly are your goals, Miss Endicott?" he scoffed without bothering to hide his sarcasm.

"To help these people, Jack." She made a sweeping gesture, encompassing the inhabitants of the camp. "To give them the basic necessities that even the poorest citizen back home has access to. Food. Water. Medicine. Those things mean life or death to these people."

"And you do that by playing war games in the jungle?"

Frustrated beyond words, Jillian looked to Gabriel for support. The hardened set of his jaw was the only outward sign that Gabriel wasn't as controlled as he appeared.

"Jillian is section leader for the World Relief Team headquartered in *Ciudad* Torisco. She and I are on a recon mission to determine the manpower the WRT will need to serve the mountain villages once the new road gives us access to the indigents now living beyond our reach."

"Or at least that's the story you're telling." Jack jammed his hands at his hips. "I still haven't heard any reason why you need a pilot. I may seem as green as this jungle, but I've lived a hell of a lot of years on a military base.

"I've been through combat drills. I know this camp is ready to pick up and move on a moment's notice. The fire and women are a nice touch, but the handguns in the bags of beans are a dead giveaway."

At Jillian's surprised intake of breath, Jack kicked the busted bag at his feet. "Now, I want some answers. Because if this is a recon mission, I'm John Wayne."

"Well, John," Gabriel replied after several tense seconds that lingered forever. "I don't know about you, but I can't go much longer on an empty stomach. We'll finish this conversation . . . after we get some grub."

Jack took a minute to consider, eyeing Gabriel like he still didn't believe a word the man had said. Jillian waited for one or the other to move, to break the silent test of wills. Jack's blue gaze seethed. Gabriel's brown one crackled and burned.

Resigned but wary, Jack finally stepped forward, scrubbing his hands down his weary face. Reluctantly, he fell into step beside Gabriel as the other man headed toward the fire at the center of the camp.

Breathing a sigh of relief, Jillian followed.

Chapter 9

With more help than was needed from the women tending to the meal, Gabriel and Jack filled their plates.

After brief introductions, and with a low-pitched wolf whistle from Rosa Garza carrying them on their way, the two men headed toward Gabriel's tent and sat on the plank stools grouped off to one side of the flap.

Jillian lingered around the fire, wanting to give Jack a chance to regroup. Accepting a tin plate from one of the women, she walked to the other side of the fire, where Rosa stirred the bubbling contents of a cast-iron pot.

"Jillian, you look well," Rosa said, ladling a scoop of potatoes from a sizzling skillet.

"Ah, wait till I get four straight hours of sleep under my belt. Then you're in for some real competition." When half of the potatoes slid from the ladle and into the fire, Jillian knew she'd hit a nerve. "Has Josh given you any trouble?"

Rosa flung her hair over her shoulder. "None. Joshua keeps Angel out of my hair."

"I appreciate you keeping an eye on him," she said, then held up one hand. "No beans or peppers for me, Rosa. I'll just stick with the potatoes."

Rosa clucked her tongue. "You're too skinny, Jillian. You'll never catch a man with those hips." Frowning, she leaned forward and, with her hands on her waist, eyed Jillian from side to side. "A man looks at you and says, 'You got no hips. How you gonna bounce my baby when you got no hips?'"

Jillian rolled the potatoes in her tortilla and thought of Jack's eyes, dropped several of the seasoned chunks and tried again. "I would hope a man would want me for more than babies and my hips."

"You're thinking maybe he'd like to be tied up with those long legs of yours?" Rosa sidled closer and lifted one artfully plucked brow. "Or taste your wide mouth before you use those lips the way a man likes?"

"I was thinking more along the lines of being appreciated for my brain," Jillian interrupted before Rosa got graphic with her description. The other woman harrumphed and stirred the simmering beans.

Blessed with flowing black tresses, she considered seduction not an art but a female obligation—one in which she found Jillian sorely lacking.

The fiery Latina swished her skirts like a mating call, tangling the yards of widow's black with the legs of her male targets.

Voluptuous to the point of excess, with a tiny waist and generous baby-bouncing hips, Rosa was a walking turn-on. No man was immune.

Not even Gabriel.

Jillian knew he and Rosa were lovers. Not openly. Their relationship was not a fact to flaunt. But it was a fact just the same. And Jillian's secret.

When her bad dreams became too much, she spent sleepless hours sitting at the edge of the encampment beneath the shelter of the trees, as silent as the creeping advent of dawn. From there she often saw Gabriel step through the flap of Rosa's tent while the rest of the camp still slept.

Rosa followed, and their parting kisses made Jillian's skin

burn: the way Gabriel's fingers roamed from Rosa's breasts to her hips and down beneath her belly, the way Rosa's hands climbed Gabriel's leg then crawled between their bodies, the way Gabriel growled and Rosa laughed.

"I'm disappointed in you, Jillian," Rosa said, bringing Jillian back. "After all these years you still think like an American."

"I don't hate everything American, Rosa."

"And you still believe in true love."

Jillian took a bite of the soft taco. She didn't know if she believed in true love or not. She had once, a long time ago, and even as much as his leaving had hurt, she would never regret loving Marco Chavero.

She wished she could see him one more time to say thank-you. But they had no contact now. It was safer this way. He had been her first lover. Her first true love. And a man who'd loved his country more than he'd loved her.

With Rosa occupied serving breakfast to two more early risers, Jillian made her escape. What she'd shared with Marco had shattered her.

After leaving him in West Palm Beach, she'd come to San Torisco, throwing herself into her work with the intent to mend. And she had—from everything but that terrible night three years later. The darkness, the fire, the drug-induced haze. And Carlos Sabastiano.

Jillian shuddered, shoving aside thoughts of a time in her life she couldn't change to concentrate on now.

"A basketball scholarship," Gabriel was saying to Jack as Jillian walked up.

Jack shook his head as he licked taco drippings from his fingers. "Never played. I ran the 440 and the 880 until arthroscopic surgery on my right knee put an end to my running days."

"I still can't believe it. You were at Baylor the same years I was at UT." Gabriel glanced up as Jillian chose the stool next to him rather than the one next to Jack.

He took a bite of taco and talked around it. "And Jillian here managed only two years at Northwestern before the World Relief Team snatched her into service. She's been down here ever since with no regrets."

"And only one big complaint," she added.

Gabriel grinned. "No bathtubs."

Appreciating Gabriel's effort at relieving the tense situation, Jillian went along with the game. "Cleaning up in a wooden barrel or a battered tin washtub is not my idea of a relaxing good time."

"There's always the river," Gabriel tossed back.

"Yeah, the same river all you men bathe in and clean your fish in—"

"At least you don't have to worry about piranhas like you did when we made that trip to Brazil."

Jillian felt the color rise to her face and avoided Jack's penetrating gaze. "Well, one day before I die I'm going to spend at least three hours in a clawfoot tub big enough for two, up to my chin in bubbles. That, and get a real manicure and pedicure."

Choking, Gabriel spewed a mouthful of potatoes onto the ground and reached for his coffee mug. "Pedicure, hell." He took a long sip. "Your pink toenails almost blew it back in the prison. I thought Jack here was gonna lose his shirt."

"I thought I was going to lose more than that listening to your macho caveman act." Jillian made a face. "You did a pretty mean impression of our dictator."

"He's not my dictator, baby." Gabriel got to his feet and waved his mug. "Either of you need a refill?"

Jack waved him off, and Jillian did the same.

"Let me grab one, then we'll get down to business."

Jillian kept her gaze trained in Gabriel's direction, uncomfortable and awkward alone with Jack. Stupid, really. She'd been alone with him the past three days.

But he'd been unconscious, and she'd been someone else, not fully exposed the way she was now. Not vulnerable. Not emotionally naked.

The thought made her tremble. That, and seeing the way Rosa spiced up Gabriel's coffee with a splash of cleavage and a pinch to his backside.

Averting her gaze, Jillian pushed her potatoes around her plate with a scrap of tortilla.

"Does that make you uncomfortable?"

At Jack's quietly spoken words, she looked up. "What?"

Jack inclined his head.

"Rosa and Gabriel?" she asked, her body warming, thinking of Jack's. "Flirting is Rosa's job. It means nothing."

"Nothing my ass. She's looking at him like a woman with a need. And you can't stand it." Jack's brow lifted. "Jealous maybe?"

Jillian shook her head. Jealousy had never figured into what she thought of Gabriel and Rosa. She was too familiar with the looks the other woman reserved for certain men.

But for the first time Rosa's expression took on a personal meaning—and prickled the hairs up and down Jillian's arms.

It was the same look Jack had leveled her way when he'd flipped her over after she'd brought him down with her whip. And again when he'd told her it was a damn good thing she was a nun. But she wasn't.

And she wondered how he felt about that now.

"Gabriel and I would never have remained friends this long if there was anything more between us."

She didn't admit that Gabriel had once proposed marriage, an offer made out of the truest sort of friendship. Or that they had slept together for a period of time when she'd been in need of comfort and he was the only one there.

"Conflict of interest, huh?"

"No. Conflict of personality. Gabriel and Rosa have a match-

ing fire. She's the type of woman he needs. He would find me
too . . . boring," she lied. There had been nothing boring about
their time together at all.

"In a pig's eye," Jack said with a snort, and moved to sit on
the stool beside her. "You've got a hot little fire of your own,
Jillian Endicott. Maybe Gabriel just isn't the right man to
burn you up."

Living and working as she did, she doubted she'd ever find
one who was—her subconscious suddenly assigning Jack the
role. The picture came to mind in clear, vivid detail—detail
too accurate to be pure imagination.

She looked up to find Jack's intense gaze drinking her in.
"What's the matter? Are you thinking of volunteering?"

The grin that curled his lip should've come with a warning.
"Just waiting for you to ask."

"Don't be absurd."

"Then don't blush."

"I never blush."

His grin grew in proportion to the wicked lift of his brow.
"The rest of the Boston Endicotts may perspire. Or color be-
comingly. But you, Jillian, you blush. And you sweat."

He reached up, briefly hesitated, then flicked a bead of
moisture from her temple. When he touched her again she
wasn't surprised, but neither was she prepared for the spark
that jumped from his skin to hers.

He moved his thumb to the hollow of her throat and jarred
loose a tear of perspiration. The droplet tickled down the
center of her chest and soaked into the ribbed fabric of her
top.

Jack traced the same path with his thumb. Hooking his
knuckle beneath her scooped neckline, he lifted the damp
cotton and blew a long slow breath against her skin.

Jillian looked up. The heat of his touch was nothing compared to the fire in his eyes.

"Why are you doing this?" she asked.

"Because you're letting me."

"That's no reason."

"Then to prove I can."

With her peripheral vision, she measured the movement of his arm. "That's childish."

"No, that proves you're not as immune as you pretend to be. And . . . that paybacks are hell."

"Paybacks?"

"You drugged me." He slid his finger lower. "Now I'm drugging you."

"Drugging?"

"I'd say you're three sheets to the wind." He skimmed down the slope of one breast, up the other. "You can't even form a coherent sentence."

"Sentence?"

"Mm-hmm. So, Jillian, how long did you scope out the job site?"

"A couple of days."

He twisted his fist in her top and hauled her close. "Why'd you slip me the Mickey in the bar?"

The face-to-face contact brought her around. She jerked away, smoothed the bunched-up fabric, and caught her runaway heart. "What do you think you're doing?"

"Taking full advantage," he nimbly replied. "Something you have down to an art."

"You won't get any answers by seducing me."

"A little seduction goes a long way in a game of espionage." He nodded his head toward the center of the camp. "I hope your friend there doesn't talk in his sleep."

"Who, Gabriel? Rosa would never betray his trust."

"A spitfire with a conscience, huh?"

"She's a loyal supporter."

"Supporter of what?"

"I think I'll let Gabriel answer that. He can decide how trustworthy you are."

"At least I don't slip drugs to unsuspecting people without bothering to find out if it might kill them."

With a deep breath of conviction, Jillian said, "As I told you before, every cause requires sacrifices."

"And yours is so noble it could require human life?"

God, if only he knew, if only she could tell him. If only she'd remained in Boston and learned how to live with her nose in the air.

"Freedom is a cause many patriots have died for. An honorable death is not in vain. Your father and grandfather both served their country. Why don't you—"

"You self-righteous snob." He grabbed her wrist. "You think patriotism requires a uniform? That I don't have my father's guts?"

Her fingers numb, her pulse thrumming in her ears, Jillian swallowed hard. "I wasn't talking about you at all, Jack. I was talking about myself."

Chapter 10

Leaving Jack hanging on her cryptic remark, Jillian walked away and joined the others at the fire. Maybe the heat from that flame was a little easier to take than the one burning a hole in her conscience.

If she had a conscience, Jack thought.

She spouted patriotism like a zealot, yet she'd kidnapped an American citizen, and a civilian at that. A traitor of the worst kind, to Jack's way of thinking. He'd never met such a scheming little witch.

Who did these people think they were? He hated taking anything from Jillian or from Gabriel, but forced himself to clean his plate. He'd need his strength to make his escape, and the opportunity couldn't come soon enough.

He might've been willing to help out a nun, but now? Uh-uh. No way.

Hell, he ought to be able to make it back to the *Policía* outpost on his own. There wasn't a doubt in his mind that those young Sabastiano guards would love to find out about this little campsite.

The face-saving gesture might even get him off the hook for the part he'd unwittingly played in the sister's diversionary masquerade.

Whatever Jillian and Gabriel were up to, it couldn't be kosher, he thought, watching as together they walked toward him. He'd play along for now. But he'd be waiting for his break. And the minute he got one, he was history.

Jillian's shadow fell over him. Jack glanced up, witnessed the contrite look she gave Gabriel, then turned away. He wasn't anywhere close to offering forgiveness.

She exhaled slowly. "I think Jack deserves some answers, Gabriel."

"Then let's start at the beginning." Gabriel settled onto the stool Jillian had sat on earlier.

"Jack, I know you were briefed on the political climate of San Torisco. It's standard procedure for any organization working with the World Relief Team. What those handy-dandy pamphlets don't tell you, however, is that Carlos Sabastiano is dictator by default."

"So who died and made him king?" Jack mumbled, not giving a good goddamn.

"Unfortunately, that's more or less what happened. Carlos assumed leadership when his uncle, Romero Sabastiano, died."

"Uncle Romero didn't have any sons of his own?"

"One," Jillian replied. "He died in a fire days before his tenth birthday."

Jack afforded her a steady glance. "And Romero played it straight. No illegitimate upstarts appeared to demand their rightful inheritance?"

Gabriel flashed a quick look Jillian's way. Jillian's gaze darted to the side, but not fast enough. Jack saw the exchange. Very interesting.

"Apparently not," Gabriel said. "No one has stepped forward, and Carlos has run the country his way for the past fifteen years."

"So Carlos was next in line as Romero's oldest nephew."

Gabriel rubbed one finger down the side of his upper lip. "No. He was the second nephew."

"The oldest died in a swimming accident years ago. Days before his tenth birthday." Jillian spoke slowly, letting every last implication sink in.

Jack's gaze flicked between Jillian and Gabriel. He slowly set his empty plate on the seat beside him. "Are you saying somebody knocked off these ten-year-old kids?"

Gabriel finally answered. "No concrete proof has ever surfaced."

"And it won't." Bitterness tainted Jillian's tone. "Even if there had been investigations, the only ones with access to the records are Carlos's own men. Do you think he would allow questions to be raised about how he came to power?"

"If I were handling a big-time cover-up, I'd make sure everything was buried, then I'd welcome a look-see." Jack stretched his arms overhead, working the kinks out of his stiff body. "An easy way to clear my name."

"It doesn't matter. The questions have never come up." Her voice dropped to a raw whisper. "He'll never be investigated."

"Other than by you two, you mean." The light dawning, Jack eased to his feet, walked ten feet away, and turned.

"Let me get this straight. In the early days of briefing, when the Smithson crew was warned to avoid certain areas where rebel guerrillas were known to operate, they were talking about the two of you and this nice, neat operation."

"It may seem that way to an outsider," Gabriel said. "We do have a lot of information not readily available to the public or the visiting press. But that's because to do our jobs effectively Jillian and I have learned to work both sides of the fence."

"So I'm not dealing with rebel guerrillas, I'm dealing with double agents." Hands at his hips, Jack rocked back on his heels. "And you expect me to trust you?"

"All we expect is for you to listen," Jillian said. "One week from tonight, the *Festival de los Santos* begins. The religious celebration is observed by both Catholic and vodoun priests.

Sabastiano's troops will be moving in over the next several days. Carlos's stand on vodoun is not a secret."

"Then violence isn't out of the question."

Gabriel shook his head. "The question of violence comes up every year, but this year will be worse. The building of the road is Carlos's assertion that San Torisco has entered the twenty-first century. He doesn't want the stigma of vodoun hanging over his head. And the San Toriscans feel their choice of religion is a sacred right."

"Enough so that they're willing to fight to the death for their cause?"

Gabriel shrugged noncommittally. "The political arena here might never be the same."

"And this is where I come in," Jack said.

Gabriel nodded. "There are two items we need to get out of the country. The timing is critical. With the increased military patrol, water is out. That leaves air. San Torisco has no landing strips, so we need a helicopter. Up and out." Gabriel made the motion with his hand. "Our associate on the U.S. Gulf Coast will be waiting for delivery."

"And you want me to fly these items out of here."

"If everything had gone according to our original plan, you would've already been there and back," Jillian replied, twisting her hands together.

Jack didn't know whether to laugh or kick the stools out from under the both of them. "You mean the plan where you scope out a job site that just happens to have a chopper pilot? Then you wait for said pilot to show up at his buddy's bachelor party?"

"Jack—"

He waved off the interruption. He was on a roll. "Now, knowing this celebration will turn into an all-nighter, the foreman has already given his crew the following day off. And since no one will be expecting to see the pilot around the job site the next day, you decide to borrow him for twenty-four hours.

"You were probably also pleased to find out that the pilot wasn't much of a drinker. Made it a lot easier to wake him up when you needed his services. The only problem I see here is that you never stopped to consider why the pilot doesn't drink. But you pretty much found that out when he wouldn't wake up after your Mickey, didn't you?"

Jack spun sharply on Jillian. "What were you planning for me to fly? No, wait. Let me guess. My own chopper? Is that how you do it in Boston, Miss Endicott? Throw a party and make the guest bring his own fun?"

"If you're finished—"

"Hell, no, I'm not finished." He turned to Gabriel. "You need a craft as big as Smithson's Chinook? Because you're outta luck if you think I'd tackle that machine without a full crew on board."

"No. Our cargo is small. We just need one able to cover the distance."

"Well, where is it?"

"You'll see it soon enough."

"I'll see it before I decide whether I fly."

Gabriel shook his head. "I'm sorry, but I can't offer you that luxury."

"It's no luxury."

"In this case it is." Gabriel's eyes darkened to a menacing shade of black. The eyes of *Comandante* Mosquera. "You go in blind like the rest of us or you don't go in at all."

"So you're giving me a choice."

"Your choice is to fly what I tell you, when I tell you." Gabriel rose to his feet. "Or, since you know your own body chemistry, you decide on which of Rosa's drugs you want and how fast you want to die."

Jack struggled for words. "You'd kill me over a friggin' cargo?"

"No, we could let you go. We'll even give you an escort back to your crew. And since you've already been reported missing, Sabastiano's men will be waiting for you. They'll take you to him. He'll question you. And then you will die the way he chooses."

Jillian chose that moment to cut in. "This isn't a democracy, Jack. You're guilty until Carlos decides you are innocent, never mind the proof. The only thing fair about your trial is that you'll get your pick of Sabastiano's lawyers."

"My trial?" He gave a wild sort of laugh. These people were lunatics. "Why would I be on trial?"

"For associating with known dissidents."

Jack raised one hand. "Wait just the hell a minute—"

Gabriel cut him off. "And for aiding and abetting a woman who, as of four days ago, has a price on her head."

Chapter 11

A price on her head.
The woman had a price on her head.

Someone wanted Jillian Paige Endicott to die.

His lungs aching to burst, Jack jetted off the sandy rock bottom of a river so clear he could see the wrinkles on his wrinkles. He surfaced, spewing and sputtering and shaking like a dog, shivering as he slicked his hair from his face.

The water had loosened most of the scab on his nose, leaving a patch of raw skin. Should he survive this nightmare, he would never forget the hell of it, thanks to the souvenir he'd be sporting for the rest of his life.

Good thing chicks dug scars.

His reflection on the water's surface mocked him with the same ugly mug he'd been living with for thirty-nine years—the one he avoided looking at in the mirror when he took a pee in the mornings, shaving blind when he bothered to do more than buzz an electric razor over his face.

Leaning back, he kicked his feet and floated naked atop the lazily drifting water, running his thumb over the gold ring that still weighed down the third finger of his left hand—a reminder that he was here against his will and that if he tried to leave there was a helluva good chance he would never see a dollar of his pension.

He knew all about facing death, seeing death, causing death, and he wondered how Jillian felt knowing the government of the country she had dedicated her life to serving had marked her to die.

What he couldn't get was what flying this shipment out of the country had to do with her life, unless she was cleaning up unfinished business, not wanting to leave anything behind should her number come up.

It was obvious that brushing up against that mortality had warped her judgment; why else the wife-pregnancy-nun routine? None of that mattered. She'd kidnapped him and put his life in danger. That was the bottom line.

And the fact that she'd been hiding the body of a call girl under that burlap sack and habit had no bearing on the here and now.

Damn.

Rolling over, Jack kicked hard and dove deep, hoping the water would calm the renegade part of his body with a mind of its own. His libido wasn't concerned with how many laws of how many countries Jillian had broken.

No, siree. Joe Bob had literally sprung to life at the sight of her sweet khaki-covered backside and the bodacious curves testing the ribs on her tank top.

Face it, J. Jackson ol' boy. You got sprung long before you saw her body. Like the first time you got a good look at her eyes.

Still didn't matter. No amount of lust on his part diminished Jillian's deception. After the baby, the wife, and the nun, he'd lost count of the number of lies, but he had no doubt that from here on the caliber of Jillian's deceit would intensify.

Governmental espionage was a big boy's game, and in the hands of a woman with a price on her head—especially a blue-blooded Boston snob with a political background—highly unstable to boot.

T.H. Endicott was a man big in stature and in convictions, not to mention in personal scandals. He didn't have a Chappaquiddick or a cigar in his past, but he did have San Torisco, the housekeeper, and her illegitimate son.

Those elements were too suspect to overlook as part of the bigger picture. Jack wasn't one to jump to conclusions as a rule, but with the congressman's recent appointment to ambassador, his past had floated like scum to the top of the political pond.

And now here was Endicott's daughter playing war games in daddy's jungle.

It was a little too convenient.

Jack wondered about the connection. Then he wondered what T.H. would think if he knew about his daughter's death sentence. Or if he did know, and his recent Capitol Hill machinations were tied to Jillian's scheme.

Facing death did funny things to people, as Jack well knew. He'd faced a lot of deaths in his life. Too many. And the prospect of facing Jillian's, no matter what she'd done to him, rankled.

"I brought you a change of clothes."

At the sound of her voice, he swam toward a small rocky outcropping that provided cover. Not that he was the modest sort. And he certainly wasn't shy.

But he was experiencing enough vulnerability that he wasn't up for letting it all hang out. Especially not in front of his kidnapper.

"Thanks," he finally said. "I appreciate it."

"Please," she said, her tone self-deprecating. "It's the least I can do after burning the ones you'd been wearing. I had no idea those would be such a bad fit. You're a lot . . . taller than I first thought."

He wondered when exactly it was that she'd first seen him. And then, treading water, his arms braced on a smoothly flat section of rock, he looked up.

She sat on the ground with her knees pulled to her chest, her arms wrapped around them, her chin resting in the crevice between.

Her eyes were cast down, as if she were studying the pebbles scattered near the toes of her heavy black boots. She looked distracted, uncertain.

Lost.

"Don't worry about it," he heard himself saying, waiting for her to react, to look toward him. The hell. He was such a sap. "They covered what needed covering."

A smile pulled at her lips and color rose to stain the skin over her cheekbones. He couldn't imagine that it embarrassed her to remember what he'd been wearing—which didn't include underwear.

Not when she wasn't embarrassed now, sitting as near to him as she was, and him not wearing anything at all.

Then again, maybe she was thinking less about his clothing and more about the way his body had felt when he'd been lying on top of her there on the jungle floor.

There in that moment when she'd taken him down with her whip, when she'd threatened him with her machete. There where her heartbeat had thundered as powerfully as his, slamming against his chest.

He pulled his gaze away, swallowed to subdue the action-reaction law of motion thing occurring even now between his legs.

Jillian Paige Endicott might have a body to die for, but the truth of her willingness to put an end to his life was the only thought needed to cool the boys.

"Was there anything else?" he asked at last, breaking the silence that had grown too tense for his liking. "I'm feeling a bit on the shriveled side here . . ."

"Oh." She jumped to her feet, turned to dust off her backside. "Sorry. I wasn't thinking."

Neither was she leaving. That much was apparent.

Jack hoisted himself out of the deep pool onto the ledge where she'd left the clean clothes. He shook off what water he could, stretching and slicking his hands back over his hair before using the thin tunic he'd been wearing as a towel.

He pulled on the briefs, socks, and fatigues and was tying the bootlaces when she spoke.

"I know no apology I make will ever be enough, but I thought it might help if I explained more of what we're facing here."

"You're not including me in that royal *we*, are you? Because the only thing I've got on my plate is making my way back to the Smithson camp."

"I can't let you do that," she said, and Jack straightened to find she'd turned toward him. Her expression was severe and intensely stoic, yet her gaze roamed over his bare torso instead of coming up to meet his. The blush on her cheeks remained high. "*We* can't let you do that. Not yet."

He didn't care what she said. She wasn't capable of stopping him; he had more than a few inches on her and close to a hundred pounds.

But . . . seeing as how he was out of his element here, he *could* use her. He could feign submission, charm her for information on where they were and how to get back to camp. That he could do.

And it was better than falling in with the rebel guerrillas, or falling victim to Stockholm Syndrome because Joe Bob thought she was hot.

He grabbed up the T-shirt at his feet and walked toward her, closing the distance between them. "I'll get back there sooner or later, Sister Jillian. You know that."

She shook her head. "Don't call me sister. I'm not a nun."

"What should I call you then? Miss Endicott? What does Rosa call you? Or Gabriel?" Jack lifted a brow. "What about the rest of your prisoners?"

"My name is Jillian. And there are no other prisoners."

"Then you're admitting I am one. I mean, if there are no others . . ."

"For now." She cocked her head to the side, softened her eyes. "If you want to look at it that way."

Uh-huh. He wasn't going down that easily, letting her get him drunk with those whiskey-gold eyes. "You tell me I have to stay here. That I can't leave when that's what I want to do. What other way is there to look at it?"

She wrapped her arms around her middle, hugged herself tightly, and sighed. The motion plumped up her cleavage in the scoop of her tank. "There's just so much at stake. I'm not even sure I can explain."

He wasn't a bad guy. He didn't want to discount what she was feeling even though she was discounting his entire experience. He wanted to give her the benefit of the doubt, or at least a longer rope to finish hanging herself.

But right now, all he had on his mind were her breasts.

"Look," she said, stepping closer, dropping her hands to her sides. "This is going to be awkward for a few days, but it'll be over soon enough."

"Not soon enough for me," Jack mumbled.

Another step. Then another. "Will a show of good faith make things better?"

"What sort of show?" he asked, tugging his T-shirt over his head and coming out the other end to find her staring.

In fact, if things hadn't been what they were between them, he would swear what he saw was interest of the come-up-and-see-me-sometime variety. Her eyes were telling him things he found himself straining to hear.

And that threw off all the ways he was trying so hard to dislike her.

She turned a half step, gestured in the opposite direction from the camp. "I'm heading out to pick up a WRT drop. Medicine and first aid supplies for the villagers. Vitamins and supplements for the team members. Things like that."

"And this is of interest to me why?" he asked, admitting his curiosity had indeed been piqued.

"I can't go alone. Esteban is going with me, but Gabriel suggested I take you, too."

"Let me get this straight," he said, thinking this sounded like an opportunity worth seizing. "Not only do you want me to fly your chopper, you want me to volunteer to do your grunt work as well?"

"You don't have to go," she said, and shrugged. "You can stay in camp."

"And do what?"

She shrugged again. "Whatever you can find to keep you busy."

"I'm free to roam on my own?"

"You'll be guarded, but sure."

"Guarded, but not under lock and key?"

"We have guns, Jack. We don't need locks and keys."

Interesting. His choices were to do nothing under the armed and watchful eye of the camp, or sign up for another trek through the jungle with Jillian and one hired gun.

He liked the odds that came with the latter.

"Do I have to wear the priest's getup again?" he asked, glancing back to where he'd left the ragtag clothes.

She shook her head. "You're a member of the WRT now. What you're wearing is fine."

This was good. This was good. He would be one against two. Still out of his element, yes, but this time he had clothes, boots, a clear head, and a clue. A weapon would've been nice, but he'd deal.

"All righty then," he said. "When do we leave?"

Chapter 12

By the time Jillian got back to camp, a clean and freshly dressed Jackson Briggs in tow, she was forced to admit the extent of the trouble she was in.

It was more trouble than she'd been in with Jack sprawled unconscious in the back of her cart. More trouble than she'd been in when he'd discovered who she was and what exactly she'd done. Even more trouble than what she'd faced when he'd tumbled her to the jungle floor and loomed above her like a man who wanted things he knew he couldn't have.

Then she'd had the safety net of her habit and disguise between them. Now there was nothing so tangible, no other symbolic *hands-off* for her to rely on and use as a shield to keep him away.

She was stuck relying on herself, and that wasn't good.

Not when Jackson Briggs stirred her blood, when he made her remember intimacies she'd forgotten, made her long for the very same and long for them with him.

It was in his eyes, something, she wasn't sure what. He had a history with as much damage as hers. A future as iffy and uncertain. Except that wasn't exactly true. It wasn't her future at stake.

It was her son's.

She checked the contents of her backpack before tossing it

beneath the seat of the same cart they'd traveled in previously. Esteban had already commandeered the back and set himself up to ride point.

If she'd been a better shot, she would've insisted they switch seats, but guns were one of the constants in her life that she would never get used to or master. She liked her whip and machete.

She did not like having no choice but to ride with Jack at her side, though having Esteban within earshot would make it easier.

Anything they talked about would have to be filtered for their audience, meaning there would be no personal conversation and no revelations.

That audience also meant there would be no physical contact except what couldn't be helped. She wasn't going to think about how narrow the seat was and how much room Jack's big body required.

"How long will this take?" he interrupted her musings to ask as she climbed up and settled in.

He followed; the cart listed beneath his weight, and she leaned with it, saved from sliding toward him by the rough surface of the seat.

It then jostled back as he wedged himself beside her, his wide shoulders taking up more than his allotted personal space. And doing way too good a job of it.

He jabbed his elbow into her ribs and said, "I mean, if it's going to take a while, I don't mind hopping in the back and giving you the extra room."

And then hopping out and forcing Esteban to shoot your cocky ass.

That was what she thought. What she said was, "It'll take as long as it takes. So the sooner we get started . . ."

"You're not blaming me for holding you up, are you?"

"If the shoe fits," she responded, annoyed by how much she let him aggravate her.

He glanced down at the boots she'd given him. "Actually, they are a little tight. But I guess I'd be pushing my luck to ask for another pair."

"Considering how many villagers there are on this island without a single shoe to their name, yeah. That would be pushing it," she said, and slapped the donkey's rump with the reins.

He grunted as they set off, the cart jerking forward. She wondered if the noise was aimed at what she'd said, or if it was just a response to the motion.

She found out at the next rut in the road.

"I'm still having a hard time seeing Congressman Endicott's daughter playing war games in the jungle."

"No one here is playing at anything. And these aren't war games. The WRT is an established human rights organization, and our interest in San Torisco legitimate."

"Okay," he said, and shrugged. "But you being here just doesn't fit."

"Fit what? Your idea of who I am? Or of who I should be? Rather judgmental, aren't you?" Not that she was particularly surprised.

Growing up in the public eye meant she'd run into opinions similar to Jack's more often than not, though she hated having strangers think they had her all figured out.

No one had ever known her that well. Not her family, her friends. Not Marco. Hell, there were times she wasn't sure she knew herself.

Times like now when she felt the pull of attraction to a man she had no business thinking of as more than the means to a very important end.

"I guess I'm a judgmental kinda guy," he said, managing to slump back in the seat and prop his crossed ankles on the board that framed the footrest. "Or maybe it's just being held against my will that's messing with my usually fair mind."

They'd traveled only fifty yards, but that didn't stop Jillian from slamming on the brakes. "It's probably best if you stay in camp then. I'll wait here while Esteban escorts you back."

"Did I say being held against my will?" He shook his head. "I meant this lingering hangover. I just can't kick the headache."

She rolled her eyes, but she did cluck her tongue at the

donkey and ignored Esteban's snicker as they started up again. "Did you ask Rosa for an analgesic?"

Jack shook his head. "After hearing about her drugs yesterday, I decided to stay far, far away from what she's selling."

"Smart man," Esteban mumbled. "Smart man."

Jillian sighed. She was regretting this trip already. "That's your call. Just don't be looking for sympathy for your pain."

"No need. I feel sorry for myself enough of the time to cover my sympathy needs." He paused a moment, then pointed down the rutted road. "By the way, feel free to drop me off at the first drugstore we run across and I'll grab a bottle of aspirin."

The man was a pain in the ass. "There'll be aspirin in the supplies we pick up. Or there will be if the Sabastiano *Policía* haven't already raided the drop."

"Does that happen a lot?"

Esteban answered before Jillian got out a single word, a long litany of rapid-fire Spanish rolling off his tongue.

She smiled to herself. "Yeah. What Esteban said."

"Uh, I caught the bastard dictator part, but that was about it."

"That's enough, isn't it? But then I figure you and the Smithson crew already know that about Carlos, as long as you've been in the country."

"You got that right," Jack said with a derisive snort. "The men weren't too happy to learn they'd be working here another year."

She hadn't heard that.

She'd been afraid the road would be left unfinished once the construction contract expired. Even charitable organizations had a rope with an end, and getting there didn't take long when dealing with Carlos.

"It's for a good cause," she said, though she doubted her words would convince him. "That should make the time pass a little easier."

"In a perfect world, maybe," Jack said and scratched at the back of his neck. "But it's hard to see the light at the end of the tunnel when day in and day out is spent working under a mother of a big black cloud."

He grew silent after that. Silent and withdrawn, as if he were feeling the darkness on a more personal level, one having little to do with the job.

She didn't want to pry, but she was curious. "Have you been down here the whole time?"

He shifted in the seat, his hip bumping hers, his thigh warm and hard where it pressed along the length of her leg. "Yep. The entire year. Off and on, anyway. When there's cargo to haul. Which I'm sure you know, showing so much personal interest and all."

She knew a lot about his work habits. What she was looking for, however, was more than his schedule. She wanted to know what kept him here.

The Smithson Engineering crew hardly needed Hank's private pilot ferrying supplies and heavy equipment to the job site. They could easily have contracted out the work.

Jack must have insisted on staying.

But why?

With a flick of the reins, she urged the donkey to the left where the trail ran smoother. "I'm just having a hard time seeing a multimillionaire's private pilot hauling freight around the jungle."

From the corner of her eye, she saw the edge of Jack's mouth lift, though his accompanying grunt clued her in that he wasn't all that happy about it. "Is this where I offer you a touché?"

"Only if it means you understand that we all have reasons for being here."

"Reasons that go deeper than the work we're doing, you mean."

She didn't respond immediately. A big, big mistake since her silence gave him a big, big opening.

"So tell me more about your reasons, Jillian. Not the big picture story you and Gabriel served up earlier. Spoon-feed me a small, intimate bite of your cause."

That was asking too much. He was looking for things she talked about to no one but Gabriel. The thought of telling them to Jack . . .

If she did, would she gain his sympathy? Would a full disclosure drive him away? Would he look at her with less hostility if he knew the truth of her plight?

She decided to start small and at the beginning. "I don't know how much of the gossip you may have heard about my father's housekeeper."

"The one he rescued during a trip here and took back to Boston."

She nodded, bracing herself as the cart dipped in and out of a rut she hadn't seen. "He'd been down here delivering private donations. Medical supplies, clothing—"

"Can congressmen do that? Privately? Aren't they always supposed to represent?"

He obviously didn't know her father well. Or was being purposefully obtuse. "My father has never been big on anyone's rules but his own."

"He probably wouldn't bat an eye at kidnapping, then."

She should have trusted her original instincts and put him out of the cart back at the camp before they'd started. Now here she was, stuck trying to make peace with a man who wouldn't give an inch.

"He may stretch the law, but he doesn't go out of his way to break it. And, no. He would not approve of what I've done." And he'd make a huge show of that disapproval. "But then, he hasn't approved of me for a very long time, nor I of him, and I'd rather not take that any further."

He didn't say anything, only shrugged beside her, the rise and fall of his shoulders brushing his T-shirt's sleeve against her bare upper arm.

Gooseflesh rose against her will and she cringed, hoping he didn't notice either response. The tension between them already bordered on unbearable.

"Anyway," she went on after finding and pulling close most

of her wits, "Marguerite came to live with us when I was five, and her son Marco and I became best friends."

"The brother you never had."

"He was, yes." She thought back to the last time she'd seen Marco, then quickly shut that window into the past. "But he was also more."

"Aha!" Jack smirked. "What did the congressman think about you hanky-pankying with the housekeeper's son under his roof?"

"We weren't under his roof," she heard herself admitting. "And besides, he didn't know. But none of that is relevant to this conversation. Marco is the small, intimate bite of my cause you asked for."

"How's that?"

"I'm here because he can't be."

"Why not?" Jack asked bluntly.

She'd been ready for ribbing and sarcasm. She'd thought he'd want to get in more digs about her father or her cause, or even rag on her some more about the inappropriate nature of her relationship with Marco.

But he'd skipped the attitude and asked a straightforward question, one she wasn't able to answer. Marco had sworn her to secrecy—right before he'd dropped out of sight after she'd told him she was pregnant with his child.

"Jillian!" Esteban whispered harshly. "*¡Alto!* Stop! *¡Policía!*"

She jerked back on the reins without thinking twice, grabbing for her backpack as the donkey stopped and bounding down from the seat.

She motioned for Jack to keep quiet and follow, her heart hammering hard in her throat as she rushed to catch up to Esteban before the trees swallowed him up.

The three of them scrambled into the thick undergrowth that encroached on the edge of the road, heads down as they stooped low and ran deeper into the jungle, crawling over downed trees, zigging and zagging when they couldn't plow through, scurrying around any clearings.

When Esteban finally stopped, Jillian was breathless. Sweat ran into her eyes, down her back, and between her breasts. The fabric of her tank top stuck to her skin.

Her knapsack weighed a small ton, her hair nearly as heavy at her nape. Esteban motioned for her to stay where she was while he backtracked to see if they'd been followed.

She didn't argue. She could barely breathe.

"What's going on?" Jack demanded, his chest heaving, his voice low but sharp.

"The *Policía* are at the supply drop, just ahead," she said, gasping as she worked to fill her lungs. "Esteban must have heard their jeeps or their chatter."

She hadn't heard anything and she should have. She should not have been thinking of anything but getting the supplies and getting back to camp.

Not about Marco. Not about her attraction to Jack.

Not about the truth of who her father was.

"What about the cart? You just going to leave it there on the road?"

"We've got to get back to camp and warn the others. We'll make better time on foot." She gripped the hitch in her side. "The longer the patrol searches for the owner of the cart, the more time we'll have to pack up and get out."

"You're taking a big risk, aren't you? Setting up shop a stone's throw from their patrols?"

"They never patrol here. Ever. There's no reason for them to be here now," she said, coming to the same conclusion as Jack seconds before he spoke.

"Then you've got a leak in camp."

Chapter 13

When they finally stumbled adrenaline-fueled and sweating out of the jungle and into the camp, they found the place in chaos.

Make that destroyed, Jack mused, changing his mind as, grimacing, he took in the scene.

So much for the Sabastiano *Policía* never patrolling this area. He'd lay odds the leak wore a long, flowing skirt and cooked a mean tortilla.

Ol' Gabriel might be sleeping with the enemy to keep her close, but Jillian denying the possibility of Rosa spilling her guts didn't make sense.

Seemed awfully blind on her part, as smart a cookie as she was.

One thing was certain. He'd been right about the camp being ready to pick up and move on a moment's notice should trouble find them.

The band of double-agent guerrillas may have lost a few tents along with the cart and the donkey, but he saw nothing to indicate they had left behind anything vital in the way of supplies or lost any lives.

Not that Jillian had noticed.

She'd exploded onto the campsite, tossing aside collapsed

tents and stacks of firewood, cooking pots, and the crude plank furniture as if she'd find dead bodies beneath.

Esteban was doing a perimeter search of his own, his gun at the ready, leaving Jack to deal with what he suspected would soon be one hysterical kidnapper.

He crossed to where she now stood near what had been Rosa's cooking fire, hands in fists at her sides, and looking lost. The hair that had escaped her bandana tie was now plastered to her face and neck.

He came close, but not too. She was already spooked. "I'm thinking we don't need to be hanging around here, you know? In case there are still patrol types lurking?"

"I don't know where they went. I need to know where they went." She didn't look at him at all, just swung her gaze around the camp.

"Jillian, hey. Step back a minute and think. It can't be safe here. We should go."

He reached for her elbow, wanting only to get her attention, to make sure she was hearing him because he wasn't kidding about hitting the road.

She whirled on him, jerking free, her eyes wild, her hand coming up to slap him.

He caught her by the wrist and twisted her around, pulling her arm up between her shoulder blades. "I'm trying to help here, Ms. Endicott. No need for violence."

"Let go," she fairly hissed, and he released her. She turned and rubbed at her wrist. "Don't talk to me about violence. It's not your son who's missing."

A son? She had a son? *She had a son here?*

He took a step back. "What do you mean? What are you talking about? Whose son is missing?"

"Mine. Joshua. He was with Rosa's son, Angel."

"Here? You have a son here? With you? Living in the jungle on the run?"

She glowered, her eyes burning with rage. "Is that a commentary on my parenting skills? Because Joshua is none of your business."

She was right. Nothing about anyone here was his business. He was only here to escape. "Where were they? Where do we look?"

"Let me think. I can't think." She rubbed her hand over her forehead, scrubbing at her worry, scraping back her hair. "Wait. Okay. Gabriel was here. Joshua knows to go to him if I'm away and there's trouble."

"That's good. That's a start." Jack waved his hand, motioning her to follow him instead of taking her arm again. They didn't need to be standing out in the open while she got her act in gear.

He headed for the edge of the clearing where the jungle grew thick. "You know the man. What would he do? The way you've run the rest of this joint, I'm sure you've got a contingency plan."

She looked up as if he'd reminded her of something she should have known all along. "His tent," she said, and made her way toward the rubble where Gabriel had been living. "If he had time, he would've left me a note. There's a hole in the trunk of the tree behind it."

They hurried in that direction, Jillian's mood picking up. She circled the tree, stomping on the thick brush at the base, and tore away bark from the trunk.

Jack waited impatiently, watching Esteban as the other man turned over the debris the patrol had left behind. The hairs on Jack's nape stood on end.

"Here it is." Jillian crashed back to where he was standing. She unfolded the scrap of paper she held. "He's heading for the point, and the WRT transport station."

"Transport station?"

She nodded. "The docks. Where the boats bring in new team

members and supplies too heavy for the drops. We should gather up anything usable we can. We're only a couple of hours behind."

"How long will it take to get there?" Jack asked, feeling his escape plan vanishing. "To the transport station."

He'd signed on for a cart ride up the road for a quickie annulment, not a trek on foot through the jungle with machine guns in hot pursuit.

She started kicking aside the detritus, searching for what she could salvage. "We won't be able to take the main roads. We'll have to be careful. And quiet. We can't afford to be caught."

She might not be able to afford it.

Getting caught, however, could be the next best thing to escaping for him.

"Oh," she said, cutting in. "If you're thinking the Sabastiano *Policía* will return you to your compound if they find you, think again."

"I wasn't considering anything of the sort," he lied.

"Good. Because I don't think you're cut out for life behind bars."

If she meant the sort of bars he'd been behind the other morning when he'd found himself in the office of the dread *Comandante* Mosquera, he'd take his chances. Had his brain been working that day, he'd already be back with his buddies.

If she meant the bars securing prisoners in the Sabastiano facilities still in use and not abandoned to the elements, he wouldn't argue. That was one fate he didn't wish on any man, woman, or child, whatever their crime.

"I'm cut out for anything," he finally said when he realized neither one of them was moving and they were both wasting time. "Even for the helluva trek through the jungle it seems is in my future."

"It's that choice thing, Jack. Like Gabriel explained about

Rosa's drugs. You stay behind, you're choosing suicide as a cure for your headache. You come with me—"

"I might as well down a bottle of aspirin," he cut her off to say.

"You won't be the first man to overdose on me," she shot back.

Jack snorted. "The others live to tell the tale? Or did they have to have their stomachs pumped?"

She narrowed her gaze, glaring at him. "You're not exactly easy to swallow yourself."

"The very reason we need to set a few ground rules for this trip."

"You say that like you think you're in charge here."

"With my life on the line? I'm not about to depend on—"

"Some woman?"

"On anyone but myself," he finished saying. "You I'll depend on to get us where we're going, but when it comes to survival? No offense, sweet cheeks, but I'm the best hope I've got."

"So it's like that then, huh? All for one and one for one?"

"I ain't no musketeer, sister. Just my own one-man army."

"That's fine. Just remember that my army was here first, and my army's in charge." She tossed him a spare knapsack. It hit him square in the chest. "See if you can find anything we might need or be able to use."

He understood that she couldn't afford to give an inch with her son's fate out of her control. He understood that because he had lived it, and he would never wish his suffering or the tragedy that had robbed him of his family on anyone.

This much he could give her, this small boon, letting her think she was running the show since her moves were the same ones he'd be making anyway, even if the outcome he was hoping for wasn't the same as hers.

After serving her a salute that had her rolling her eyes, he scrounged through the camp for supplies, finding two small knives, a pair of wire cutters, and a handheld pinball game he slid into his pocket instead of the pack.

For the next couple of days, they'd be living on whatever food was grubbed up in the tins she'd snagged, and on fruits and edible tree bark.

Maybe they'd feast on a fish or two if they happened by the river and he rigged them a line.

How bad could it be, living off the land?

She knew her way around the island. She'd been immersed in this life for a lotta years.

All he had to do was follow her lead—that and *carpe* any chance to get back to Dodge that fell into his lap.

Hell, if the shipwrecked *Swiss Family Robinson* could make a go of it, having his own personal guide made him golden.

Chapter 14

Golden had been too optimistic a word. It was a damn sweltering pigsty out here.

The bandana he'd tied around his head was drenched, sweat dripping off the fabric and into his eyes.

He wasn't about to complain, what with Jillian ahead of him silently soldiering on, and him not relishing looking like a wuss.

She was a helluva strong woman, both physically and mentally, doing what needed to be done and staying smart every step of the way. She had yet to make a move or decision he'd felt might be the wrong one.

Of course, she knew where they were going, and he had absolutely no clue, but there was more to her confidence than her sense of direction. She'd been doing this guerrilla thing a while, and it showed.

He could tell by the way she pressed forward, always alert, never hesitating over a change in direction, never ending up with a low-hanging branch in her eye, never sinking up to her ankles in fetid jungle muck.

And it wasn't like he was some kind of sissy metro boy who hated the thought of getting dirt under his nails, or breaking a sweat outside of the gym.

Hell, look at what he did for a living, the places he had to fly into, the scrapes he had to dig himself and the SG-5 operatives out of.

In fact, the last time he'd sat behind a desk had been during his aeromedical training.

But damn if Sister Jillian didn't know her way around the great outdoors.

And if she wasn't the sexiest thing ever to wear army boots, then he'd been downloading the wrong photos.

Her body was tight and compactly muscled, and she made use of every bit of it as she moved, ducking and dodging and sidestepping all the roadblocks he ran into.

Then again, if he were keeping his eyes on the trail instead of on the way her triceps flexed when she shoved aside the branches and knocked shoulder-high plants into his way, he wouldn't be needing bandages to go with the aspirin he had yet to get his hands on.

It was just that thinking about what Jillian-not-a-pregnant-wife-or-a-nun might look like naked was a whole lot more palatable than thinking about her forcing her own kid to live this kind of life.

If she wanted to bang around in the jungle wearing cartridge belts over her chest and a machete at her hip, that was one thing.

But to make her kid endure this craptastic existence was one hundred percent something else.

She had a family rolling in dough and connections living in the States. All those advantages at her fingertips, yet she'd dragged the boy into the middle of harm's way.

And it wasn't like Jack didn't understand wanting to keep close the fruit of one's loins, to watch the kidlet take his first steps, ditch the training wheels, hammer his first inside-the-park home run.

But that wasn't what was going on here, and he didn't need to know more than he did to recognize the truth.

There was no way this was about Jillian doing what was best for her son. In fact, he couldn't imagine it being about anything but her selfishness.

She'd wound up drowning in some big kettle of stinky fish and wanted someone around to remind her that she wasn't alone. He understood that, too, even though he very much was. Alone.

He'd chosen not to drag anyone into his hell, but then his kid had died in the same accident that had taken his wife, and that had made it easy to step onto the high moral road.

Speaking of roads, he needed to stop and take a leak, and see about refilling his canteen.

Hopefully Jillian knew where to find water that wouldn't use his insides later for any sort of revenge.

He picked up the pace and hurried to catch her rather than calling out her name and ending up with his mouth duct-taped shut.

She wasn't kidding about keeping it quiet. Earlier, she'd glared a hole through his midsection to his spine when he'd been unable to hold back an atomic sneeze.

He caught up and tapped her on the shoulder. She whirled on him, her whiskey-gold eyes burning with a hatred that stopped him in his tracks.

"What do you want?" she spat out on a whispered hiss.

He did a mental double take to see if he needed to go anymore, or if she'd scared the piss right out of him. Hmm. Nope. Still there.

"Give me fifteen seconds." He reached for his zipper and lowered it. "You can watch or you can turn around. It's just that I don't relish the thought of being stranded without a compass to my name."

She huffed, crossed her arms, and presented him with her back. He took care of business, tucked himself away, and decided to worry about more water after he got to the bottom of whatever was making her mad.

They had days to spend together. This wasn't going to work out so good if they couldn't get along.

He tapped her again on the shoulder but kept his distance so he didn't lose a limb.

"What now?" she asked without turning.

"Can we take a minute?"

"Just make it fast."

He felt his cheeks heating. "Uh, no. I mean, I'm done here. I want to talk."

She spun around and glared. "What part of quietly and quickly do you not get? We don't have time to talk. Especially since our conversations turn into arguments that get way too loud."

"Why do you think that is?" he asked, not liking the answer he came up with.

She tied the bandana holding back her hair tighter around her ponytail. "What did I just say, Jack? This isn't the time for a Q and A."

He shook his empty canteen. "I need water."

"You've emptied that already? No wonder you keep having to stop."

He'd stopped once. "What? It's hot. I'm sweating. It wasn't full to start with." He could see the steam coming out of her ears when there was no need. Her response had crossed the line from *reaction* into *over*. "Besides, this is your backyard, not mine. I need time to acclimate."

"I told you. We don't have—"

"Time. I know." She was nothing if not a broken record. "But you can't tell me taking fifteen minutes now to refuel won't save us thirty down the road when I pass out and you have to do mouth-to-mouth to revive me."

He had her there. He watched her expression shift from dark to not so, watched the fight go out of her on a long exhalation of breath.

Watched as she hung her head and accepted the inevitable and what he'd known all along.

He was right.

"There's a spring that feeds the stream we've been following. It's not too far."

The fact that they'd been following a stream at all was news to him, and sent a volley of *Swiss Family Robinson* points into her corner.

He'd been too busy breaking leaves and bending stalks and snapping twigs, marking the path, to notice that they were indeed climbing steadily upward.

"Then let's go," he said, adding, "quickly and quietly," just to get a rise if he could.

She dropped back so they could walk side by side, his thigh bumping her hip every few steps. "I meant what I said, you know. You really are a pain in the ass."

"Comes naturally. Like my good looks and charming personality."

"You argue. You give me a hard time. You're always wanting your way. What part of that is charming?"

"What? Nothing about the good looks? The tight ass? The killer smile?"

"If you're fishing for compliments, give me something to help us get to where we're going and I'll think about it. Or at least find me a six-pack I can drink, because as nice as they are," her scarred brow came up, "your abs aren't doing me a bit of good."

Ha, he mused. But she had noticed. And he wasn't above using that physical attraction as leverage, or seduction as a weapon.

He could hardly forget the way she'd responded to the touch of his finger when they'd been sitting in front of Gabriel's tent.

And he'd take the memory of her body tumbled on top of his there on the jungle floor to his grave.

He shook off the thought and found another nudging into its place. Something she'd said about having cut off all contact with her family.

He wondered how that played into her decision to drag her kid through the jungle.

"As long as you've been down here, I would think you'd have figured a way to get the things you need. Even if it meant getting it from your family."

"I told you. I don't talk to my family."

"Ever?"

"Ever."

"A bad estrangement?"

"You could say that."

"What about your son?"

She slowed, her voice tightened. "What about him?"

"Doesn't he want to see his grandparents? Don't they want to spend time with him?"

She came to a stop. She turned. She didn't bother to cloak the emotions in her eyes. "My son is my business, Jack. Not yours. Who he sees. Who he spends time with. None of that is your concern, okay?"

Her voice, her words, both were deceptively calm. But her eyes. They gave her away. He sensed an explosion, and because he was who he was, he pushed.

"Why play violent video games when you can live one, eh?"

She swung. Her fist flew toward his jaw, a full right hook that answered any question about whether or not she hit like a girl. She didn't.

But he knew how to duck, and so caught the blow on the shoulder and spun to the side, grabbing the whip and machete from her belt as he fell.

The momentum she'd put into her swing sent her stumbling forward, and it took only a well-placed boot tangling between her feet to put her exactly where he wanted her.

On her back. On the ground. On his good side.

He hooked his leg over hers and flipped himself up to straddle her hips, grabbing her wrists, binding them with the whip and pinning her down.

Her chest heaved, and her eyes burned with a volcanic fire, searing him with all the fury she'd convinced herself her circumstances demanded be kept bottled up.

She was the hottest thing he'd had beneath him in longer than he could recall, and his body didn't care about the severity of her crimes.

"Don't ever hit me again," he said, breathing hard, weighing this chance he had against never having another, wondering about the cause of his hesitation before his mouth came down.

He hadn't knocked her to the ground to kiss her, but no way in hell was he going to stop. She tasted too damn good. Sweet and wanting and chili-pepper hot.

He stretched out on top of her, his legs bracketing hers, their hips pressed tight, their tongues tangled.

She didn't fight to free her hands or struggle to dislodge him. All she did was kiss him back, her mouth wide open, the whimpers caught in the back of her throat vibrating in her chest.

Oh. God. Damn. Joe Bob down below was knocking on heaven's door, and heaven had yet to say no. In fact, Jillian was doing nothing to turn him away.

She arched her hips into his, brought her head up off the ground as if desperate to kiss him harder, moving to his cheek, his earlobe, his neck.

He kept her wrists pinned beneath one of his hands and brought the other down between their bodies, tugging up the hem of her tank top and finding her skin.

And then he stopped. She tasted like the best kind of candy, and her softness reminded him exactly how much he missed having a woman in his bed.

But he could tell by the sounds she made that she wanted

something more than he had in him to give, and that made what they were doing insane on more levels than he could count.

And so he stopped, trying to catch his breath and force his blood back into his veins. His ears were ringing, and he couldn't find his voice. Not that it would have done him any good; he couldn't think of anything to say.

And then Jillian realized she was the only one still involved. She stilled, lowered her hips and turned her head, looking anywhere but at him.

He knew he should roll away and let her go, knew there should be something he could say to help her blow off what they'd done as inconsequential.

Except he knew there were consequences out the wazoo they'd both have to face, and so he said nothing at all.

Instead, he waited for her to break the steamy ice, waited for the rhythmic pounding of his heart to return to its usual calm, waited, waited . . .

Chapter 15

"Do you hear that?"

She couldn't speak. She couldn't look at him. She couldn't move. Oh, Lord, what had he done to her, and why had she let him?

Worse than let him. Asked him for more and given him so much.

"Listen," he said, then asked her again, "Do you hear that?"

He let go of her wrists and sat up, straddling her legs while she freed her hands from the coil of the whip. Dirt clods and twigs and a tree root were digging into her shoulders. She hadn't even noticed.

God, she hated that she'd let him see her like that, and she started to snap at him to get off. She got as far as pushing up onto her elbows and opening her mouth before he pressed a finger to his lips.

When she finally heard what he was hearing, she wanted to crawl even deeper beneath him. It was a sound she'd hoped to never hear again. One that made her chest ache. One that made her twitch and shiver.

"Do you hear that?"

She nodded, still shivering.

"Do you know what it is?"

She nodded again and felt his gaze roam over her when she didn't say more.

"Are you going to tell me?"

She started to shake her head but knew he wouldn't let her get away with not talking to him. Besides, it was way beyond time to face her past.

"I didn't know we were so close. I should have known. I should have paid attention to where we were." She should have done a lot of things but she'd had Joshua on her mind, and Jack on her heels, saddling her with guilt and desire.

"What exactly is it we're close to?" he asked, rocking back on the balls of his feet to stand, then offering her a hand and pulling her up beside him.

She dusted off her shoulders and backside, cringed as she dug an insistent rock from her thigh, avoiding his gaze all the while. "When we were in the cart. Before we reached camp. Do you remember coming across the *Policía* outpost? And how easily you frightened the guards?"

He lowered his voice to match hers. "You said something about them thinking me a voodoo priest."

"Right."

He frowned, shook his head. "No way we're back at the outpost already. I may be all kinds of confused about directions on the ground, but time I'm good with, and I know we haven't had enough to make that return trip."

"We're not back at the outpost." If only they were. "We're close to a clearing used by the local voodooists for their ceremonies."

"That's where the drums are coming from?"

She nodded. "We're going to have to backtrack and cut around."

Jack didn't immediately agree. "Cutting around, sure. We can skirt the edge and stay out of their way. But backtracking will throw off your schedule even more."

More than stopping to kiss me? she wanted to ask, but bit her tongue. "If we don't backtrack, I'm not sure we can swing wide enough to avoid being heard."

"If they're not locals and not Sabastiano's goons, does it matter? Aren't they the ones your relief team is here to relieve?" Jack stepped around her and grabbed up his things. "I'd think they might provide the same in return. Maybe even a weapon or two." He shook his empty canteen. "Or water."

"It's not that simple." She did not want to get into this with him.

Explaining what she knew about the cultists' ceremonies and how she knew what she did would be like willingly sliding a knife between her ribs to her heart. "We can't just go in and ask for their supplies and leave them without."

"I didn't say anything about leaving them without," he said, his frustration rising. "It just seems like we'd be wasting a resource if we don't at least try. It's not like we have a whole lot of others."

"We have what we need," she insisted. She was not going to set foot near that clearing. Not one foot. "Let's just go before it's too late."

"Too late for what? Jillian, you're not making any sense. We need water—"

"We can't, all right? It's out of the question." She hated feeling so flustered. Hated dodging him when she could just lay out the facts and be done with it.

Except she hadn't yet figured out, these nearly ten years later, how to be done with any of what had happened to her that night, since she could remember only certain parts, and the ones that were missing were critical.

He stood there staring at her, clearly thinking she was a mental breakdown waiting to happen.

And oh, if that didn't make her want to laugh because of how right he was, and how close she was, and how successful she'd been at lying to herself all this time and telling herself she was okay.

Jack came close and hovered. "Are you going to let me in on the joke? Because if there's something funny going on here, it is way the hell escaping me."

Obviously her expression had given her away. And she thought herself so stoic. "You know that fine line between love and hate? There's another one between humor and hysteria, and I'm not doing such a good job straddling it."

He continued to hover, but his gaze grew less stony. "I told you we'll catch up with Gabriel and your son soon. But you've got to hold it together until then. And that means thinking straight. If there are villagers nearby who might be able to lend a hand—"

"No. No." She wrapped her other arm around herself and hugged tight.

They had to get out of here. They had to get out of here now. "Trust me on this, Jack, please. Asking for help of any kind, even for water . . . we just can't. Not from these people."

"Jillian—"

"We're leaving. I'm not saying anything more." She backed up a step.

"Wait, Jillian." He held out one hand, but she wasn't going to let him stop her.

Shaking her head, she turned to grab her backpack from the ground—and ran into whoever it was standing behind her that Jack had been trying to warn her about.

Chapter 16

Jack was getting more than a little bit tired of Jillian's secrets. It wasn't that he was a stickler for telling all. But the truths Jillian seemed intent on keeping to herself were putting him in all sorts of danger.

He and his camel were running out of straws.

Here he was, already dealing with being kidnapped and working on getting back to his life by making this trek through the jungle, when along comes a big fat blast from her past in the form of interpretive dance, designer drugs, and bondage.

Talk about being slammed out of left field.

He'd had *no* idea what they were in for when Jillian had turned and plowed into the native he'd been trying to warn her was there. No idea at all.

The guy had materialized out of thin air, if Jack were to continue with the clichés, and he hadn't been alone. None of the crew had been dressed in the Sabastiano *Policía* uniform, but he hadn't had time to ask if that was a good thing or bad.

The moment Jillian had started to take him on—and damn if she wasn't gutsy, ramming her shoulder into his midsection, her knee into his balls—the guy's posse had appeared to quash her, grabbing Jack before he could mount a similar defense.

Once the bunch had produced weapons that appeared to be

Sabastiano issue rather than courtesy of the humanitarian WRT, he'd given up arguing about going along. He'd trudged after Jillian, his wrists bound behind him, the leader's band of brothers bringing up the rear.

Their little troop hadn't had to walk far. As Jillian had said, they were close.

Now he understood what it was they were close to, and why she'd been trying to get him to move quickly and quietly away in the other direction.

She'd told him yesterday a bit more about what he'd already learned during his time in the jungle. The religion practiced by the locals who hadn't been "civilized" by Carlos Sabastiano had been uniquely personalized by the indigenous San Toriscans.

Now that he was getting a firsthand look at this small congregation's "services," Jack decided it was also a religion that wouldn't play with the devout along the Bible Belt.

His hands finally untied, he sat cross-legged on the ground in front of a bonfire. Jillian sat similarly at his side, her fingers twisted tightly in her lap, her head hung low, her chin tucked to her chest.

Two of the guards stood behind them. The rest had joined the villagers in worship.

With the fire spitting orange sparks, and plumes of white smoke feathering against the dark sky, the natives danced around the flames in a follow-the-leader circle.

Men and women both, and both of all ages, wore the sort of tattered clothing Jillian had given him to wear as a make-believe priest, making him wonder what sort of priest she'd disguised him as exactly.

The worshippers held drinking cups made of bamboo, cups that always ranneth over as they were constantly refilled by the nut job running the show. He was dressed much like the others but was better accessorized.

Strings of bone and wood trinkets clinked around his ankles, knees, neck, waist, elbows, and wrists. Jillian had whispered to Jack earlier as the dance had started that the fashionista was the cultists' priest.

Remembering the Damballah-Houngan-Loa bit that had gotten them through the Sabastiano outpost safely, even though he'd been short on the costume jewelry, Jack wanted more of an explanation.

But all she'd had time to tell him before they'd been ordered into silence was not to swallow anything they were given to drink. He could fake it, spit it out, pretend to nurse the drink for hours, whatever. But he needed to trust her on the not-swallowing thing.

He didn't have to be told twice.

Between his own chemical intolerance and the effect of the drink on the dancers, he took Jillian's warning to heart. It was imperative that he keep his mind clear and focused on Jillian, her son, and their safety.

Except it was really hard to watch the party going on and not think about that kiss. About the softness of her skin, the softness of her lips, the soft way she whimpered to get what she wanted.

And it got even harder not to think about all that when the drink dissolved what was left of any fireside inhibitions and the dancers' clothes began to fly.

The woman closest to him backed into her bare-chested partner's body and covered her own naked chest with their joined hands. They pinched, they rubbed, they massaged the fleshy weight of her breasts as if auditioning for a role in a porn flick.

Jack felt his throat and his chest and his other things tighten, and he tried to look away. But sex was happening everywhere he turned except for the one place he most wanted it to be.

He cast a quick glance to his side and found Jillian's head bowed and her eyes closed. Her face and the skin above the scoop of her tank top were flushed. He would've attributed it to the heat of the fire if her chest hadn't been rising and falling like a bellows.

And if her nipples hadn't reminded him of gumdrops.

Sex and candy. Jillian was making the two inseparable in his mind, and all they'd done was kiss.

That kiss was giving him hell. There had been tongue and teeth and torturous want, and she hadn't even cringed at having the jungle floor beneath her. All that dirt and squishy ripe foliage and who knew how many bugs.

None of it had bothered him, but he'd been on top and bothered in another way, a way that was bothering him again now just looking at her skin in the firelight, at her hair in damp ringlets clinging to her face.

He wanted to get back to where they'd been, to see how far they might go, to ignore everything about why either of them thought getting naked was a smart thing to do, and just bump and grind themselves silly.

She still hadn't looked up, and he wanted to tell her not to, to look straight at him—only at him, nowhere else—if she felt the need to open her eyes, but was pretty damn sure she was keeping them closed for the very reason he wanted to.

While he'd been staring into the fire and thinking about kissing her again—and thinking that he'd be more than willing to let her get on top and take the brunt of the jungle floor himself—what had been a lot of groping and fondling had become a whole lot more.

The women had dropped to the ground on all fours, their necks arched and heads back, their breasts swaying to the rhythm set by the men pounding into them from behind.

The priest continued to make his rounds, only instead of plying his people with drink, he'd switched to smoke, sucking on what looked like a bong, then blowing the intoxicant into the faces of the copulating couples until a pungent haze hung low over the clearing.

The whole thing was just too weird for words, yet Jack couldn't look away. His heart was beating hard and his breathing was labored, and he didn't want to talk about the party in his pants.

He started to move, to scoot over in front of Jillian to block her view of the goings-on, but her hand shot out to clutch his thigh and stop him.

"Don't move," she whispered in a voice he barely heard, but her warning came too late. He'd caught the notice of the priest, who until then seemed to have forgotten they were witnessing his X-rated production—an act no doubt deemed equally perverted by Carlos Sabastiano.

With drums pounding from the far side of the fire, the priest walked slowly toward them, the whites of his eyes glowing, his dilated pupils glossy and black, his nostrils flaring as if he'd scented his prey.

Jack wasn't too keen on filling the bill, especially when the predator was stoned out of his mind in the name of religion and enforcing his beliefs with guns.

The priest motioned for Jack to get up. He did, and he stepped in front of Jillian. The priest used the bong's column-like chamber to push Jack aside.

It was a gentle push, a nudge, though Jack didn't doubt the man had it in him to get a lot more physical, considering the arsenal he had backing him up.

But the whole situation was unnerving enough that, instead of moving, Jack locked his gaze on the priest's and reached down to offer Jillian his hand. She took it, clenching tightly to his fingers as he pulled her up and not letting go once he had.

The priest then motioned to one of the guards standing behind them. Jack watched with wary regard as the man ducked through the door of the small hut that was the only structure in the clearing.

Moments later, before Jack had time to do more than cast a

quick glance at Jillian and squeeze her fingers to remind her he was there, the guard returned with two cups of the ceremonial drink.

The one Jillian had told him not to swallow.

The one that had the dancers rolling and writhing, humping and heaving.

The guard thrust the cups into their hands and wouldn't take no for an answer. Jack met Jillian's gaze, prepared to follow her cue.

While the priest sucked on whatever it was burning sweetly in his pipe, Jillian lifted the cup to her mouth with both hands and pretended to drink.

Because he was watching closely and wasn't flying high, Jack saw the liquid dribble down her chin and neck and into her cleavage.

Her forearms blocked the priest's view and that of the guards. And with a sheen of sweat already glowing on her skin, the dampness the drink left behind would take a close inspection to see.

Unfortunately, he was too intent on Jillian and not fast enough on the draw to get away with the same ploy. By the time he raised his cup to drink, all eyes were trained on him as the drums rose in a crescendo.

He'd fooled two members of the Sabastiano *Policía* into thinking he was a Latin-speaking voodoo serpent. How hard could it be to trick these goons?

He upended the cup and, chemical intolerance be damned, emptied the liquid into his mouth.

Jillian gasped, her eyes wide and filled with more fear than he'd seen her display, a fear that nearly choked him into swallowing the drink.

He recovered and held her gaze, bringing the back of his hand to his lips to wipe them while he gently spit the drink along his arm, giving her a quick wink as he did.

The drink left a fruity taste in his mouth and his tongue

buzzed before it went numb, but the relief in her eyes was what he noticed most.

At least until the priest blew his smoke into both of their faces and he gagged.

Before he'd recovered and drawn a clean breath, he and Jillian were dragged into the fray. He didn't know whether to rejoice or rebel.

Getting his hands on Jillian was enough to make him groan. But not here. Not like this.

What he wanted was not for public display, but was a private fantasy he'd give up before ruining by making it a part of this freak show.

Besides, whatever it was going on here was something that was getting to her in ways he didn't understand—and wouldn't understand until they could talk.

And that wasn't going to happen until they put this place behind them.

Which he wasn't sure was going to happen any time soon now that the priest was coming at them with a rope and a knife.

Chapter 17

It was like revisiting the past, and Jillian was more than a little bit spooked.

She'd been here before, done this before, wanted more than anything to shove what she knew about these people and her experience with them out of her mind.

But what she wanted and what she was going to get weren't the same.

She didn't remember the knife and the rope, but the fire, the dancing, the drink, and the smoke, those she would never forget.

Neither would she forget the sex.

The mindless orgy nearly indistinguishable from this one. The women on their hands and knees. The men taking them violently from behind.

The pleasure so obvious in all of their faces, in the sounds they'd made, the moans and the cries.

The sex she'd engaged in, however . . . She couldn't remember a thing. She knew it had happened. Her body told her for days after that it had.

But her mind didn't want to admit she'd been a participant in an act that went against the core of who she was.

She had no problem with sex. She had no problem with kinks or fetishes or public displays of affection.

If these villagers—the very ones she was here to help, the very ones Carlos Sabastiano claimed were a blight on his country—if these villagers chose to worship their deities in ways foreign to her, who was she to pass judgment?

But when they forced their customs and beliefs on outsiders? That was when her problems began.

Ten years ago, she'd still been new to the country and naïve enough to think helping these people meant she would come to no harm.

She'd warmed herself by their fire. She'd been transfixed by the spectacle of their dance. She'd graciously accepted the ceremonial drink she'd been offered and never suspected a thing.

Gabriel hadn't thought to warn her before she'd set off to deliver medical supplies that morning. He'd been the one to find her two days later, her clothes torn, her body bruised, her memory mostly gone.

The aftereffect of the drug in the drink he'd explained two days too late.

That was when he'd taken her under his wing.

To this day he still carried the guilt of failing to keep her safe, still hated letting her out of his sight. He made sure they were partnered on all WRT assignments and swore when she brought her son to the island to lay down his life for the boy.

Joshua had thrived under Gabriel's influence just as she'd thrived beneath his protective eyes. But she felt he had given her too much of himself in his efforts to take the blame.

Later, it had been maybe a year, once she'd returned from her trip to the States after Joshua's birth, she and Gabriel had become lovers.

Physically, they'd given each other so much, but the emotional connection had been strained. They'd looked too hard for something that wasn't there and agreed in the end that they worked best as friends.

She wondered what her friend would think if he could see her now, her hands laced on top of her head, her body bound to Jack's.

The priest had wound the harness around their waists, in and out of their legs, looped it beneath their armpits and over their shoulders, pulling the rope tight enough to flatten her breasts on Jack's chest.

She was glad that Gabriel wasn't here, couldn't see, and would never have to know. His guilt at not keeping her safe would only exacerbate her fury and embarrassment—the emotions both self-directed.

She was furious for loving the feel of Jack's body.

She was embarrassed that her nipples were hard enough to let him know.

It had to be because of that kiss.

She couldn't think of any other reason she wasn't struggling to get away. She needed to get away. To get to the rendezvous point and meet Gabriel and make sure Joshua was safe.

But getting there meant making it out of here in one piece. She would be of no use to her son if she ended up dead.

She knew from her own experience with the smoke and the drink that the revelers would wind up unconscious at the end of the night.

If she and Jack could hang on until the wee hours of morning, they could make their escape without being seen or having to put up a fight.

She had to think ahead, to focus on their flight.

And she had to keep avoiding Jack's gaze—not an easy task with her arms now around his back, and his around her waist; and with men and women under the influence of the ceremony, the sex, and the mind-altering drugs surrounding them.

"Hi," Jack said, looking down.

"Hi," she said, staring back.

"I'm guessing it's safe to talk now."

"It's safe enough," she said, and tried to shrug.

He cut his gaze quickly around the clearing. "I noticed there wasn't a lot of effort made at precoital conversation."

She felt herself smiling. "That's because they swallowed. And that was very well done, by the way. Spitting out what you had in your mouth."

"My tongue feels like a gauze bandage," he said, smacking his lips.

She remembered thinking the same thing after Gabriel woke her up. "It'll get better."

"You have experience with whatever it was we were given to drink?"

"Unfortunately, yes."

"You want to tell me about it?"

She closed her eyes, shook her head. She couldn't have that conversation right now. She didn't want to be having any conversation right now.

But as close as they were and as out of it as everyone else was, she saw no reason to wait. Except maybe the part about them being in such a compromising position.

And the fact that her stomach started heaving when she thought about the past.

"Sorry about this, by the way," he said, as if reading her mind. "I can't say this hasn't been a fantasy of mine since you knocked me flat with your whip, but this isn't how I saw it happening."

"How did you see it happening?" she asked, her eyes fluttering open and the words tumbling out before she could stop them. And she'd thought the other conversation was one best avoided.

She took a breath and sighed because it was impossible to shrug when so tightly trussed up. "Never mind. I just . . . never mind."

"I'll save it for later," Jack said, a gentleman letting her off the hook. "Right now I think you should tell me what you can about what's going on here so I'm prepared for what we're facing. You can leave out the personal stuff. Just give me the Wiki version."

"Wiki?"

"Wikipedia. The free online encyclopedia?"

"Think about who you're talking to, Jack."

"Yeah, yeah, jungle girl." His hands on her rump squeezed and teased. "Just give me a quick recap. And pretend that you don't feel any of what's going on behind my zipper. Because no matter his training, Joe Bob has a mind of his own."

"Joe Bob?"

"Seems a good name for the rowdy sumbitch. Neither he nor the boys have any manners at all."

She hadn't thought anything he might say could make things better. She'd been wrong, and it was hard not to laugh. "I'll ignore Joe Bob if you'll pretend I need my headlights to see."

His mouth quirked, and he flexed his fingers again where his hands were tied. "It's late. It's dark. Works for me. Now, what's the story?"

She wondered why he made it so easy to keep a light heart, and to tease when she should be panicked. The concern about Joshua was there, front and center. She felt the pressure weighing heavily around her heart.

But Jack helped dispel her fears by refusing to show any of his own, or to even take the cultists seriously.

Despite the road that lay ahead, he made her want to smile, and for that she owed him the truth. She'd give it to him. She just couldn't do so now when she needed to stay focused on the present.

Though she remembered little of what had happened to her, she knew the cultists would soon succumb to the drink the way she had.

When that happened, she and Jack had to be ready to go.

"Since they left our clothes on," Jack began, prompting her, "it's pretty obvious they're not expecting us to do it like the mammals on the Discovery Channel. So we're trussed like a turkey why?"

She wondered if she'd been tied up before. She remembered the bruises and soreness. Scrapes on her palms and her knees, yes. But nothing about ropes.

"Unless they're using close contact to get us in the mood," Jack continued. "Which would be a lot more effective if they'd stripped us first."

The picture he painted had her blushing. "Shh. Don't give them any ideas."

"Do they speak English?"

"It doesn't matter."

"What, you'd rather not chance having to rub up against me?"

"I am rubbing up against you," she said, eyes narrowed and grimacing.

Jack wiggled both brows. "Yeah, but unlike everyone else here, we're still wearing our pants."

Grr. "Have I ever told you what a pain in the ass you are?"

"Several times, but it's worth the name-calling to see you smile."

"I'm not smiling now," she reminded him.

"You should. You look great when you smile."

"I only smile when the situation calls for it."

At that, Jack barked out a laugh. "And you don't think the absurdity of this one does?"

Pain in the ass. Pain in the ass. *Pain in the ass!* "It's not absurd. It's very real and very serious."

"Laughter is still the best medicine."

"Goddammit, Jack. Will you stop with the platitudes!" she ordered, wanting to stomp her foot but fearing the rope would ride up and pinch her.

"Hey, just keeping things upbeat. I don't want you to give in to the panic I see in your eyes."

"It's not panic."

"Whatever. You're not focused. I shouldn't have asked about the past because you're thinking too much about what happened to you then instead of what's happening now."

What was he saying? All she could think about was getting out of here.

"Look at me, Jillian. Look at *me*."

She did.

"The details. Not the big picture," he said, his voice soft, his eyes encouraging. "Think about one step at a time. Start with getting us out of these ropes."

"No. If we try anything, they might see," she said, though she knew he was right. She'd been thinking too far ahead, planning beyond the moment when they had yet to get free.

"I don't mean right now. But we need to be ready. I think I can reach the knot above my wrists. If I loosen that one, you should be able to take up the slack at my neck and untie the one that's bruising my shoulder."

She patted as far as she could to the side, fingertips grazing the rope, felt him testing the knots in the small of her back. "Okay. Now what?"

"Now we watch and wait and hope they do that passing out after sex thing and cut us a break."

Her mouth twisted. "You mean that man passing out after sex thing."

"Don't tell me you've never passed out," he said with a snort.

"I stay awake. I cuddle. I do not pass out."

"Sounds to me like someone is protesting too much."

"I swear," she muttered under her breath. "Next time I kidnap a pilot, I'll check into his chemical intolerance *and* make sure he's mute."

"That'll make it hard for him to communicate with the control tower."

"We don't have one."

"Hmm," he mumbled, losing the sarcasm. "You never did tell me what it is I'm flying out of here."

"I think we covered that already," she said, relieved that he seemed to have accepted his fate. She didn't know what she would do if he didn't.

She had to get Joshua out of here now, before the *Festival de los Santos*.

"Are you going to miss me?"

The question took her aback. "What? You mean when we're not all bound up?"

"No. When I'm gone. I'm flying out of here, remember? And I'm sure as hell not flying back."

The chopper he'd be flying belonged to Carlos Sabastiano. Jack didn't know that, and never would.

The loss of the aircraft would help cripple the dictator further. Jack didn't know that either, and never would.

Neither did he know how much trouble he was going to be in when he was found with the helicopter Stateside.

But, yeah. She would miss him. More than she wanted to admit to herself, and she sure wasn't going to admit it to him.

"I'll take that as a yes."

"Take what as a yes? I didn't say anything."

"Your silence speaks volumes."

"My silence was all about not wanting to hurt your feelings," she lied. It wasn't his *feelings* that were going to be hurt.

"You kidnapped me, Jillian. You don't care about my feelings."

"Okay, now you're just making me mad."

"Good. Now use that fury to help get us out of these ropes."

What? She glanced around and saw that they were the only ones still conscious, or at least still upright.

She felt Jack's hands scrabbling around behind her, felt the rope harness go slack, and got busy at his neck with her end of their deal.

Chapter 18

Jillian didn't slow down until they'd covered at least a mile. Crashing blindly through the jungle meant a lot of noise Jack knew she didn't like making.

But he also knew they needed to put as much distance as they could between them and that place—and as rapidly as possible.

He would quiz her about the whole shebang once they'd caught their breath and calmed down. Or maybe he'd wait until they reached the rendezvous point and she knew her son was safe.

Then again, with Gabriel present, she might decide she had nothing to say, and Jack didn't want to go through all this and have that happen.

Call him a nosy bastard, whatever. He wanted to know more about what Jillian had been through.

He told himself it wasn't because of the sex, but he knew that was more than a little white lie. She didn't practice voodoo. She'd obviously been forced into something, or been drugged and unaware.

He wanted to know what had happened because of the marks it had left on her. This life she had chosen. The fact that she had brought her son here to raise. Her separation from her family and Joshua's father. That was all the stuff of an emotional upheaval.

He knew that because of his past with Mandy and Justin, how he'd withdrawn from life, quitting his job, selling his things, packing up, hitting the road, working for food and a roof overhead when brutal weather made sleeping outdoors, well, brutal.

It was during that time that he'd met Hank Smithson, or had run across one of Hank's SG-5 operatives who wasn't in much better shape. Christian Bane had been undercover, of course. Jack had just been down on his luck.

It was a down of his own making, sure, but that hadn't stopped him from lending a hand and bailing Christian out of a bind. Doing so had resulted in a job that better suited the tightrope that was his emotional state.

He'd gone to work with men who understood that telling chaplains or psychologists every detail of why you were living out of a duffel bag and working for your grub didn't make the reasons go away or the nightmares stop.

He recognized the same in Jillian. How none of her choices had made things better. How talking to him wouldn't change a thing about what had happened. That didn't mean he couldn't lend a hand.

When he caught a branch across his face so hard it left a stinging welt, he put down his foot. Enough. His body hadn't seen this much abuse since boot camp, and they'd covered plenty of distance for now.

He surged forward and grabbed her arm, pulling her to a stop. She turned to face him, her hands going to her hips, her chest heaving, her eyes wide and picking up a glint of light from the very bright moon.

He bent forward, sucking in air and willing away the hitch in his side. When he straightened, he caught her gaze and watched her inner hell break loose.

She was in his arms before he braced himself fully, and he stumbled when they made contact. He stepped back into the tree trunk behind him, wrapping her up close.

The bark was smooth, the branches low. It was the perfect cover for their kiss: the tongues, the teeth, the breath that was hot and damp. And for Jillian's hands, which were beneath his shirt, at the button of his fly, reaching into his pants.

"Hey, hey." He pulled his mouth away from hers far enough to mumble. He wanted her to stop and think, not to mindlessly strip him down.

Liar, he told himself. Mindless suited him just fine.

Still . . . "Jillian, hey, slow down."

She pushed his shirt up to his armpits, shook her head as she moved her mouth to his chest. "I don't want slow. I want fast and I want now and I want to forget it all. I want you to help me forget, Jack. Please help me forget."

He wasn't so picky about why she wanted him. He just wanted to make sure that she did. That she wouldn't regret it later. That she wouldn't turn on him when all was done and slap the skin off his bones.

"If you're sure," he said, pushing away his curiosity about what was eating at her, if it was more than what they'd gone through tonight.

"Yes." And that was all she said.

She dragged the flat of her tongue over one of his nipples, kissed her way to the other side through the fur on his chest, teasing him, arousing him, her hands twisted into fists in the fabric of his shirt.

They had their knapsacks and the clothes on their backs, nothing more. No extra shirts to roll into pillows or lay on the ground like blankets and sheets.

He had no toothbrush, no washrag. No condom. He barely had the sense to push her away, but he did.

"We can't do this, Jillian, baby, wait." He gripped her shoulders, set her away with enough of a shake to jar her back to the here and now. "It's not safe. We can't—"

She shook her head almost violently. "We can. No one is going to find us."

"Not that kind of safe." Being found was a worry that hadn't even registered on his radar. "I don't have a condom. We can't."

She reached for the hem of her tank top and pulled the shirt over her head. Her bra came next, a slinky number out of place with the rest of her survival gear.

He wondered about her panties, wondered about the fullness of her bush, wondered about his sanity because he was nuts for wondering about anything but getting to where they were going.

But then he forgot about everything when he realized her breasts were as heavy and round as he'd imagined, as mouthwateringly creamy as he'd known they would be. Her nipples were dark, like hard chocolate centers.

And safe or not, he wanted her.

She tucked her top and bra into her fatigue pockets and came close. "I'm the safest thing you'll find in this jungle, Jack. I won't be giving you anything but a very good time."

He wasn't worried about diseases so much, but he'd been a father once. He wasn't going to be one again. "No babies? Because I'm shooting live rounds—"

"No babies. No diseases." She splayed her hands over his rib cage. "As long as *you're* clean . . ."

He'd bathed in a river hours ago and had been sweating like nobody's business. But considering they were both in that particular boat and his blood work had been stellar for years, he grabbed her by the waist, lifted her up, and backed her into the tree.

Her legs came around his waist, her arms around his neck.

He buried his face in the valley between her breasts, breathing her in.

She smelled like sweat and like sugar and like fire, and she tasted like a starving man's feast.

He sucked at the plump flesh, biting her, licking her, his hands slipping down to cup her ass as he moved to draw a nipple into his mouth.

She gasped, arched her neck, threaded her fingers against his scalp and held him there. His cock swelled, his balls tingled. He widened his stance and tilted his hips, settling her spread thighs against him.

They both groaned, and suddenly nipple wasn't enough. He wanted to suck on her clit, her pussy, to drive his tongue into her hole and taste her. He wanted to finger her, to fondle her ass, to fuck her. He wanted to turn her inside out before shoving his cock down her throat.

Before he could figure out how to do any of that without letting her go, she was tugging at his shirt from behind, pulling it over his head. He had to juggle her from arm to arm to get it all the way off, but her weight was nothing when compared with his need for skin to skin.

She was soft, her skin smooth and supple. She was warm, but it wasn't enough. He needed what was between her legs, and so he lowered her feet to the ground.

Once she was standing, he went to work on her belt and her zipper, sliding his hand into her pants and her panties the second he had room.

Her moisture seeped from her swollen sex and he spread it with two of his fingers, sliding one on either side of her clit and using his knuckles to squeeze. He dug deeper, and when he pushed inside, she whimpered, tightened around his fingers, and ground her clit against his wrist.

She returned then to his pants, shoved them halfway down his ass and lifted his cock and balls free. He groaned, his chest rattling, and groaned again when she dislodged his hand and dropped to her knees.

She took him into her mouth, her thumb and forefinger ringing his shaft just beneath her lips. He braced his palms against the tree and leaned forward.

The darkness and the shadows made it impossible to watch, so he used his imagination and just felt.

She worked him like a pro, as if there were nothing that would give her more pleasure than sucking him to the back of her throat, toying with the slit in the head of his cock, rubbing the ridge of the mushroom cap and the bulb of the head with her tongue.

He couldn't believe this was happening, that she was giving him this, that he was letting her. He didn't want to think she was blowing him out of guilt. He didn't want to think he was letting her because she owed him for the hell of the last few days.

He wanted this to be about need and desire and the attraction that had seethed between them since she'd whipped him to the ground and he'd rolled on top. And he knew it was because of the way he wanted her, because of the way what she was giving him wasn't enough.

He grabbed her by the shoulders and hauled her up, leaving his pants down and reaching for hers. She bent to get rid of one of her boots, slipped out of that pant leg and turned, her hands flat on the tree trunk, her legs spread wide and her ass in his lap for the taking.

And so he took, stepping in behind her and dipping his knees. He held his cock in one hand, held her hip with the other, worked himself up and down through her pussy's slick heat and shoved deep, stopped, shuddering as sensation soaked in and the echo of her cry slowly stilled.

Then he began to move, thrusting in and out, reaching around to apply the pressure her body told him she wanted against her clit. He rubbed and stroked. She wiggled her hips and ground against him, reaching between her legs to find his balls and lightly squeeze.

He thickened inside of her, pulsing, his heart beating, his balls aching and telling him it was time. He released her hip to toy with the bud of her ass, pushing against it, slipping his finger inside.

"Yes," she hissed, whimpering. "Please, yes, oh yes. Please, do me there. I want you."

Her pussy was tight, but her ass was tighter, and her moisture made the perfect lube. He pulled free of her sweet cunt and pushed against her anus, easing slowly inside as she begged.

She was incredible, so hot, so sexy, amazing in the way she knew what she wanted, in the way she didn't hold back but growled at him and begged.

He slid a hand between their bodies and pushed two fingers into her swollen sex, playing her, stroking her clit with his thumb, making love to her pussy with his fingers, making love to her ass with his cock.

He'd never known a woman this uninhibited, this hungry, this greedy about getting her way. He couldn't say no. How in the hell could he say no, when he'd never thought he'd feel this way again?

And then she came, taking him with her. She contracted around him everywhere, and her spasms milked him dry. He was empty in seconds, the pulse of his cum explosive.

He finished and pulled free, turning her as he sank to his knees, holding her hips, opening her sex with his tongue, licking through her folds, pushing inside of her, sucking at her clit, bringing her to climax again.

She was salty and sweet, his candy, his chili pepper. She was hot, she was sexy, she was . . . his. He couldn't deny that truth any more than he could deny that dealing with it was going to change his life.

Chapter 19

They dressed without speaking. He started to say something a couple of times, but she stopped him. She couldn't deal with talking right now. She had to process what they'd done.

No. What she had done. What she had let him do. What she had invited him to do.

Where in the world had that come from?

She liked sex, loved sex, had opened herself up fully to Marco and Gabriel both, giving her body to both men, giving her heart to only one.

But she'd trusted both not to hurt her or use her, not to think of her as a nympho slut for the things she'd wanted them to do.

She'd wanted the same things from Jack, and she didn't understand why. She didn't know him well at all, certainly not well enough to trust him the way she'd trusted the only other men she'd made love with.

It made no sense at all that she wasn't satisfied, that, in fact, she wanted more.

And the worst part of the whole thing was that she was deceiving him on so many levels, using him for her cause, and that she would toss him away like she would a disposable lighter once Josh was safely away.

He followed as she led him toward the river where they'd been headed before being detoured—How many hours ago was it? How many hours had they lost?—by the cultists' guards. She knew said guards had been on the lookout for Sabastiano's patrols when they'd interrupted her argument with Jack.

Forcing the two of them back to the clearing was as much about the cultists' self-preservation as was keeping them there for the show. And after that tussle with the guards, and with the sex and the smoke and the sweat lingering on her skin, a bath was definitely in order.

She could only hope a good dunking would clear her head, because it was obvious she was as muddied upstairs as she was exhausted.

She needed to be thinking about getting to her son, not about how much easier it was to deal with her worry over Joshua because Jackson Briggs was around.

"Jillian, hold up," he said from just behind her shoulder.

She slowed enough for him to catch up and match her stride, but she didn't look at him. She didn't want to see his face and wonder what he was thinking about her, about what they had done.

"Look, we've got a way to go before hooking up with Gabriel, right? You may be used to this pace, but I'm still working your drugs out of my system. I'm going to need to sleep."

Finding a place to bunk in for the night she could do. And sleep? Anything to keep Jack from talking worked for her. "There's shelter ahead."

"Good, because we need to talk."

"No, we don't," she said as the riverbank came into view.

"Plans, Jillian," he said, his impatience clear. "We need to re-group, decide if the delay hurt us. I figure the sex will work itself out when it's time, but we need to talk about what we do next."

"Fine. We'll talk when we get there."

Using the light of the moon and the sound of the running water as a guide, she followed the river upstream another quarter mile or so to the small falls Gabriel had showed her months ago. The WRT used the natural cave behind to store emergency supplies.

As far as she was concerned, this constituted just that—whether they used the supplies or not.

"The rocks are slick," she called to Jack. "Watch your step."

"Yeah, yeah, jungle girl. Give me a flashlight and I'll watch yours, too."

His grumbling brought a grin to her face, the first one she'd felt tease at her lips since the last smart-ass thing that he'd said. She liked that he made her laugh. She needed to laugh.

"I might be able to do just that," she said. "I might even be able to scare up a tin of crackers to go with the canned meat we brought from camp."

"Canned meat, yum." He made a gagging sound. "Guess it would be too much to hope you could scare up peanut butter instead."

She ducked around a trickle of water at the entrance to the recess and stepped inside. "We'll see."

Running her fingers along the wall, she walked deeper into the mountainside's small cave, feeling the crunch of gravel beneath her feet and stopping when she found the sharp, shelf-like outcropping.

She reached up, breathing a sigh of relief when she felt the tight seal of the small plastic box there. Sensing Jack behind her, she opened the container and lit a match from the supply inside.

The flame nearly blinded her as it flared, but her eyes adjusted as she lit the wick of the small lantern tucked safely toward the rear of the shelf.

"There," she said, adjusting the flame and securing the chimney. "Now you can see where you're going."

"I can see a whole lot more than that," he said, hefting his backpack to the ground. "Where the hell are we?"

She followed his gaze around the small grotto. "Esteban and Gabriel found this place when scouting the area before we camped. They stored a few things here as a just-in-case precaution."

"Just in case you found yourself on the run from a freaky voodoo priest?"

Jillian dropped her knapsack and headed toward the rear of the cave and the trunk of supplies that she knew included a bar of soap and a blanket. "That wasn't true voodoo, you know."

"Then what was it?" Jack asked, joining her, hovering as she checked the labels on the various cans.

"No crackers, sorry." She handed him a tin of peanut butter and a tongue depressor. "What you saw is exactly what Carlos Sabastiano is trying to get rid of."

"Tha withh docthor sthigma," he said, his mouth already sticky and full.

She went back to digging in the trunk. "The villagers are cut off not only from the civilized world but from their own past, too. They've lost many of the traditions they brought with them and will do anything to try and connect to the gods they fear have abandoned them."

Including killing firstborn sons before they turn ten, she thought to herself, *thinking that will keep the ruling line pure.*

"If their gods got wind of that ceremony, no wonder."

"I saw it ten years ago. Then I knew nothing about what was happening, or why." She stopped, not wanting to stumble through an explanation that would have him wondering what all she was leaving out, not wanting to think about Joshua's upcoming birthday.

"What *was* happening? And why?"

. . . but a general query she could deal with. "It's a fertility dance."

"Fertility? As in having babies?" He sounded almost panicked.

"Not just babies," she said, shaking her head. "The harness is about binding together the land and the livestock and the people. Yoking together everything they have that can be used to pay homage, or show respect and devotion, or offer up as a sacrifice."

"Then how come we were the only ones tied up?"

That she didn't know. "Don't ask me. I have a hard time believing their ancestors took things so far. In fact, my research shows it would have been out of character for them to do so. But now their lives are so hopeless . . ."

"And desperate times call for desperate measures?"

"I know. It's disheartening that it's come to this. That even with the efforts we've made, we haven't been able to do more. That we haven't been able to save them."

"From Sabastiano? Or from themselves?"

"I'm not sure there's a real difference," she said, closing the trunk and turning to sit, the bar of soap she'd wanted in hand. "If he hadn't focused solely on the people living in *Ciudad Torisco*—"

"You mean, the ones who make him look best on TV?"

"Exactly," she said, thinking how her father had used that same medium toward the same end, and how both men's actions had influenced so many of her own.

It was easier to think about how tired she was, and how she didn't have to think of either man when asleep.

"If Carlos hadn't turned his back on those clinging to their heritage, who knows if we'd even be here now? The villagers might have the roads they need already. And have access to the basic necessities so many of us take for granted."

"You don't seem to be taking anything for granted," Jack said after finishing his peanut butter, breaking the silence that had settled between them.

The smell made her stomach rumble, and she was as ready

for food as she was for sleep, a bath, and the change of subject.
She looked up to find Jack looking down. "What, because I
managed to shake any sense of entitlement I was born with?"

"Were you? Born with one?"

She snorted. "I'm a Boston Endicott, remember? Blue blood,
silver spoon, even a framed certificate showing my lineage and
the entitlement into which I was born fully vested."

He clicked his tongue. "Must have been a hell of a childhood."

"It was," she said, missing that innocence, that perfectly
unspoiled life. "But then there's a reason it's said that ignorance is bliss."

"So, who phoned in your wake-up call?"

"My father," she told him with a snort. "Though he has no
clue."

"Good ol' T.H.? No way."

Even appreciating Jack's sarcasm, this part she couldn't re-
visit while sitting down. She needed to move, to keep her
hands busy before she crushed the soap into crumbles.

She got up and headed for the small fire pit, where she read-
ied the kindling. "I came home for Christmas after my first se-
mester at school—"

"Northwestern, right? In Chicago?"

"Right. Marguerite, our housekeeper—"

"The one your old man took back to the States for medical
care after seeing her injured here?"

"Right," she said, waiting for another interruption. When
none came, she went on. "He cut through the red tape and
took care of all the paperwork they needed to stay in the
States."

Jack leaned against the cave wall, crossed his arms over his
chest. "And what about that made him the enemy?"

She shook her head briskly, dispelling his assumption that
her break with her father had anything to do with the strings
he'd pulled.

"That all happened a long time ago. Marco and I grew up together, so the wake-up call wasn't about what my father had done for them. It was about what he'd done *to* them. Or to Marguerite. What he'd apparently been doing for years."

"He was sleeping with her. Cheating on your mother and doing the help."

Astute man. "Yes, but it was more than that." She took a deep breath. "If he'd been having an affair with Marguerite, that I could understand. Not condone, because it would still have been adultery, but my mother never had been an . . . affectionate woman."

She waited for a snide comment about the distance she had obviously fallen from the family tree, but he said nothing, and she offered him a silent thanks. "What my father did to Marguerite was beyond unforgivable. He kept her prisoner. A sexual prisoner. He forced her to service him. I walked in and saw things . . ."

She shuddered. All these years later and she still couldn't believe the truth of those years. Or of what she'd seen, and the absolute terror in Marguerite's eyes.

"And that's why you're here?"

It was more than that, but those events had been the impetus. Her father trotted out the Chaveros to prove his humanitarian nature and raped Marguerite once the lights and cameras were off.

She nodded. "Marco and I found her papers, and he took her away. I told my father what I knew and what I had seen, and the evidence I had proving what he had done, and told him if he ever contacted her again, I'd give the information to the press. Then I joined Marco in Florida, left school, signed on with the WRT, and came here to work."

"That was when?"

"Thirteen years ago."

"And you've been down here all this time?"

"I went back to Florida for a few months." She stood. The

fire pit was ready. The soap was safe to use. Her stomach had almost settled. "Marguerite died, and I spent some time there with Marco."

"But he never came back here with you?"

"He can't." Her almost-settled stomach heaved. "It's . . . complicated."

"Even though he's the father of your son?"

Chapter 20

"I'm not going to talk to you about Marco or my son," Jillian said, stripping down to her panties and bra after giving him a long stony stare.

"I'm going to take a bath. I'm going to eat. And then I'm going to sleep. We've got a long two days ahead of us. I suggest you do the same."

Jack watched her go, glanced at the pile of clothes she'd left on the cave's floor, then shucked down to his bare ass and followed.

The woman didn't want to talk about her past lovers or her son, yet she'd opened up physically with no prompting at all. And he wasn't supposed to care about any of this? He wasn't supposed to be involved or interested?

Well, no. He wasn't. Except he was. The latter part anyway. He wasn't quite ready to cop to the whole involvement thing. That was too close to commitment for comfort.

But how could he not be interested in what made her tick after she'd begged him to screw her brains out? And no, that didn't make him shallow. It made him a man.

And the fact that he was standing naked in a cave while having these thoughts was hardly lost on his Neanderthal self.

He hadn't been in a real relationship since Mandy. He figured he'd blown his chance for true storybook romance, since he was responsible for the death of the only woman he'd ever loved.

And he sure wasn't about to fall for his kidnapper in any sort of emotionally meaningful way—no matter how intrigued by her he was.

That didn't mean he couldn't enjoy her body. Or seriously appreciate the fact that she wore plain cotton on her bottom half and silk on top.

Or the fact that she had balls the size that she did, blackmailing her own father, the inimitable T.H. Endicott, hypocrite and perv.

Jack wasn't one to judge any man's sexual druthers, but what the congressman had done did indeed go beyond the pale. Jillian should have seen her father sent away for good, but Jack knew when it came to sex and politics, the scapegoats took most of the blame.

The childhood abuse, the substance abuse, the forgivable lapse of judgment, and the media's distorted eye. All of those factors played into public sympathy and compassion, no matter how undeserved.

And then as he ducked out from behind the curtain of the falls, Jack's whole train of thought derailed. Jillian was walking out of the water to the edge of the bank, slicking back her wet hair and showing him everything she had.

He headed toward her because, really, there was no way he was going to stop, just as there was no way to hide Joe Bob's reaction.

She saw him coming and stilled, stiffened, her gaze dropping to his erection that was long past half-mast.

He didn't say a thing, or look away. Neither did he stop. He walked right by her and into the blessedly cool water, kept walking until he was in over his head.

He stayed that way until he couldn't breathe, then shot to

the surface, glad to find most of his blood back in his veins where it belonged.

When he shook his head and cleared his eyes, he found Jillian disturbingly close, the much-coveted bar of soap in her hand.

He started to reach for it but stopped because he couldn't help himself. "Are you going to stand there all night or put that to use?"

"Are you going to stop asking me questions about my son?" She turned the soap over and over, lathering up her hands.

"Son? What son?" he heard himself saying while not promising her a thing. He might be a horndog, but he still had his wits and knew not to fold his hand.

But Jillian was nobody's fool. One of the things he most admired about her.

"That didn't sound like a promise to me," she said, backing up so that the water level fell to her waist . . . then using all that soap on her tits.

"I promise to stop asking you questions about your son." But not about Marco.

"And about Marco."

"Fine. And about Marco." But not about your family.

"And nothing else about my family."

He suddenly understood how kingdoms could be surrendered for a hot piece of ass.

She was standing there, pinching her nipples, lifting her breasts and squeezing them, palming them, pulling at the centers and inviting him to share.

It took a whole lot of will to find his voice and sell his soul. "Your family is off-limits. From here on, you volunteer what you want, and the rest is strictly need-to-know."

"Then let me tell you what you need to know, Jack," she said, her voice husky. "I have been celibate so long I might as well *be* a nun. So if you are at all interested in having me give you a bath, then it would be more of a pleasure than you can imagine."

No. He could imagine. He hadn't slept with anyone but his own right hand in a year.

Even during the trips he'd made to the States to work with Hank's organization that saw a different sort of action than did Smithson Engineering, he hadn't gone to the effort to do any hooking up.

Call him a nosy bastard, whatever. But since having what he'd had with Mandy, he was no longer a fan of nameless, faceless sex. He liked it with personality, and kidnapping or not, Jillian had personality in spades.

"Jack?" she prompted when he hadn't taken a step either toward her or away. Her tone wasn't quite as confident as before.

Hard to believe he had that effect on her, or that she could be nervous about anything after what they'd already done.

Then again, it wasn't like they'd been in a position to cuddle after sex, and he hadn't done a damn thing to let her know that she was one fantastic fu—

"Jack?"

"Yeah. I'm interested. Just chilling the goods so they won't be too hot to handle."

Her laughter shimmied up from a place deep in her throat. "Thanks for the concern, but I've felt your goods, and I can deal with the burn."

Ha. "It's not you I'm worried about."

"So, you get overheated. It's not like we don't have the rest of the night."

"We don't. Not if we want to sleep," he said, regretting the words when he saw her close down.

She stared at the water's surface, trailed her fingers across it, creating tiny ripples. "Every time I close my eyes, I see Joshua's face. As much as I need to, I don't think I'll be sleeping tonight."

He was in front of her now and though she was naked and

wet and slick with soap, it was her eyes that drew him. He saw how sad she was, how miserable. He saw more worry than he'd realized she was suffering before.

He took the soap from her hand and wrapped his arms around her, holding her while she shivered, a reaction to her thoughts and not driven by the temperature of the water or that of the breeze.

"I can do this myself," he said. "And then we can get back and build a fire, and rest even if we don't manage to sleep."

"No. You need sleep. And I want this. To touch you. To pleasure you."

"It would pleasure me more if you would think about yourself instead of me."

She slid her hand down to his and took back the soap before he could stop her. "I am thinking about myself, Jack. I am ruthlessly selfish when it comes to sex."

He wasn't sure what to think. What move to make. Whether to give her what she told him she wanted, or whether to listen to his instinct that told him all was not right in Jillian's world.

In the end, the caveman won the battle. Joe Bob could look at her body and think about her being ruthlessly selfish for only so long without the boys turning blue. "Are you saying not getting any has exacerbated that tendency? Because that seriously works for me."

"I need to be mindless for awhile," she said, moving close enough to work up a head of suds in the center of his chest. "That's not too much to ask, is it? Having you take me away?"

He'd take her anywhere she wanted to go as long as she didn't stop what she was doing to his nipples with her thumbs. He lifted his arms, laced his hands on top of his head, let her play. "Where do you want to go?"

She slowed the circular motion of her hands just briefly before starting up again with the sort of bath he could get used to, lathering his shoulders, his biceps, his armpits, his neck. "Back to the cave is sounding good to me."

He wasn't going to disagree, but he liked the idea of a round of water sports first. "So, now you're in a hurry?"

"I don't have to be," she said, moving to stand behind him. "I can go so slow you won't be able to stand it."

"Promises, promises," he ground out, as she got to work on his back, kneading the base of his neck and the muscles along the full length of his spine.

"Fine," she said, her fingers slipping between the cheeks of his ass and probing where he didn't think he'd ever been probed before. "Let's see who cries uncle first."

Chapter 21

Jillian had no idea if she'd be able to outlast Jack, and quite frankly, she didn't care. She needed a senseless distraction, and he was the perfect stranger, making her feel so damn good.

And then there was the fact that *he* felt good. His skin, his muscles. His skin. She could touch him for hours, kneading, stroking, teasing the parts of him that responded so obviously to the pleasure.

She'd missed this sort of soothing tactile contact as much as she'd missed the more intimate moments shared with a man. Feeling a penis hard and thick inside of her was a sensation that nothing else equaled.

That didn't mean her palms and fingertips didn't tingle at the thought of discovering all the textures of a man's body. The parts that were smoothly resilient, the parts that were covered with hair or stubble. The parts that hung loose but then tightened.

And she already knew she would miss being with Jack once she no longer needed him and he was gone.

She palmed his buttocks, slipped her hands beneath to his thighs, massaging him there before sliding her hands between and pushing his legs apart. He tensed, and she soothed his skin, calming him and laughing softly when he remained as tight as a steel girder.

"You'll never win anything at this rate," she teased.

"Depends on what you call winning," he said, his voice pitched low and as stiff as the rest of him. "And I don't think you heard me say uncle."

It felt so nice to have a reason to smile. And a chance to toss his own words back at him. "Your body's talking a whole lot louder than your mouth."

"My body's been in dry dock for months. It's having to ease back into things slowly." He shuddered, cleared his throat, and shut up.

That wasn't at all what she'd expected, that he wasn't one to slip into the back room with one of the girls at the Cantina Mañana as so many of his coworkers did.

And he obviously wasn't too happy to have admitted that much, judging by the way he'd clenched his buttocks at the same time he'd zipped up his mouth.

As if she were going to be deterred by either when she had him where she wanted him.

She cupped his balls with one hand, rubbing the swollen extension of his erection that ran behind with the fingers of the other. "So you were telling *El Comandante* the truth then. About not testing the local waters."

He tightened up his muscles even more. "One-hundred-proof, eighteen-karat, sure-as-shooting truth."

"Too busy working to get laid?" she asked, coaxing him to relax. "Or nothing strike your fancy?"

"Oh, my fancy's been struck," he said, sucking in a sharp breath when she teased his ass. "But I've never been the love-'em-and-leave-'em sort. Besides, look at how much trouble I almost got into without ever unzipping my pants. Imagine what might've happened if I had."

Her imagination chose to go elsewhere. If he didn't love

'em and leave 'em, then what was he doing with her? "A cautious man."

"Yeah, well, I've got my reasons."

"Ones you want to talk about?" she asked, sloshing water up between his legs.

He shuddered. "No more than you want to talk about *your* family."

His celibacy had something to do with his family?

She thought back, searching for anything she'd learned from him about his life and his loves, and drew a blank beyond the fact that he was a military brat and a hell of a good pilot.

Now she was curious, but she was also having too much fun with his cock and his balls and his tight little ass to toss a bucket of cold water into the mix.

Her questions could wait, and if she never got her answers, would it really matter in the scheme of why he was here? No. It wouldn't.

And she needed to stop going there before her guilt grew to consume her.

"I don't think I want to talk about anything at all," she finally said, slipping her arms around his waist, splaying her palms low on his belly, taking him into her hands to stroke.

His erection bobbed upward at her touch. "And here I thought I was going to have to remind you of the many other things you can do with your mouth."

Cocky bastard. Did he know that she *was* dying to taste him again? To feel the way he responded to her tongue? She released him and stepped away, crooking her finger when he glanced back to see where she'd gone.

The water swirled around her hips and her thighs as she headed for the cave, listening to the rustle of the leaves in the wind, the crystal-bell sound of falling water, and the echo of Jack's frustrated growl.

She was barely out of the water when he scooped her up,

cradling her in his arms and against his chest. His skin was cool, his breathing shallow.

She laced her fingers behind his neck and held on as he carried her, nipping and nibbling on the parts of him within easy reach.

He tasted like the soap she'd used to bathe him, citrusy herbal and sweet, and like Jackson Briggs, so unique and unexpected, the man who was making it very hard to keep her emotional distance.

His heart beat with a powerful rhythm, pounding against her hip. And he moved with a purposeful stride, as if her weight was nothing, as if she didn't burden him at all.

But his strength was in more than the muscles he used to carry her up the embankment. He was strong enough to understand what she needed from him, and that she couldn't give him all the answers he wanted.

She knew that because of their uneasy truce and all the things he wasn't telling her either. Things she shouldn't want to know about him but did.

Wanting to know anything contradicted everything about why he was here. She shouldn't want anything except to lose herself in the pleasure he gave to her body.

Yet when they reached the cave and he lowered her to the blanket covering the hard dirt floor, she knew that was only part of the truth.

Jack left her there, propped up on her elbow watching him stir up the kindling already stacked beneath the firewood in the pit.

He found the matches on the lantern's shelf and struck two, a smile on his face as the flames began to lick at the dry tinder.

"Why the smile?" she asked, unexpectedly breathless at how beautifully the fire's glow highlighted the contours of the muscles in his hip as he squatted and shifted on the balls of his feet.

"I was thinking that this would be a good time for that magic fire dust you used to incinerate my clothes."

"I like this fire a lot better."

"Why's that?" he asked as he joined her, lying down to face her, draping an arm over her hip and pulling her flush against him.

He was warm and solid, and so very aroused. "I like the light. The way it flickers on your skin. Shows off your body quite nicely."

"Into voyeurism, are you?" His eyes glittered with the reflection of the flames.

"I am." She nodded. "I gave up prim and proper and decorous a long time ago."

"Prim and proper is highly overrated. Decorous sounds too highfalutin. I like my women hot and sweaty and down to earth."

"The women you bed, you mean," she added for a reason she didn't understand. "Not the ones you might wed. Double standards, and all that."

"Actually," he said, his eyes dreamy, "my wife was quite the hellcat."

Jillian swallowed hard. He'd had a wife? "You were married?"

The thought bothered her. It shouldn't bother her. Why did it bother her? And why hadn't he told her before?

That would be because you agreed not to talk about your families, you moron. You don't want to talk about Marco and Josh. He doesn't want to talk about—

"What was her name?"

Jack's eyes narrowed. "Mandy, and she's in the past, while we're in the present, okay?"

She nodded again. Mandy. A sweet name. A prim and proper decorous name. Mandy didn't sound like a hellcat.

"Jillian?" His hand moved from the small of her back up

her spine, massaging all the way to her shoulder blades and the base of her skull.

"I'm here," she said, shaking off the past that didn't matter and scooting closer, rolling onto her back and looking up into his face. "I'm here."

"Physically, maybe." He reached up, brushed her hair from her forehead. "But you're thinking about Mandy instead of thinking about me. Mandy died a long time ago, so I'd rather you think about me."

She closed her eyes. He'd had a wife, and his wife had died, and he was here making love to her.

It overwhelmed her. The hurt they'd both suffered, the damage they shared. And to have found each other here, in this place, with the way she'd treated him, the things she had done . . .

She could have killed him, giving him Rosa's drugs. He could have died, and she would have buried him, and she would never have known him. Neither would she have known him if her plans had not gone awry, and suddenly—inexplicably, tears welling—she was so very glad that they had.

He started to leave her, shifting up to sit on one hip and turning his stark gaze toward the fire. She'd been quiet too long. She knew that. But there was so much here to take in, to put into context, to turn over and over the way Joshua might examine a bug.

Later, she told herself. Later. Right now she needed Jack. And even more amazing was the realization that Jack somehow needed her.

She reached for him, his shoulder, then his arm, and waited until he'd turned toward her before she tugged him down. His resistance, already minor, crumbled when she smiled, and he came down on his hands and knees above her, straddling her, his eyes searching hers.

She didn't know what he was looking for, but she met his gaze without moving, never flinching, waiting until he was satisfied, until one of his brows lifted and the corner of his mouth quirked into the hint of a smile.

"Are you better now?" she asked.

He frowned. "Better?"

"Better now that you're back from wherever it was that you went."

"I am if you are," he said, giving her no clue about what he'd been thinking.

It didn't matter. She wasn't going to guess. She knew, and she didn't care. All she cared about was making sure they both had a good time.

Starting now.

Chapter 22

"Crawl up here," Jillian said, tapping her lips with her finger, teasing him with a flick of her tongue.

She didn't have to ask twice.

Jack made his way up her body, parking his knees on either side of her shoulders, the arrow of his cock pointing straight to her mouth.

He watched as she opened up and took him inside, shifting his gaze between her eyes and her lips as she sucked him. He tempered the thrust of his hips, not wanting to choke her, but damn, he could not stay still.

She ringed his shaft with one hand, and sweat burst in the small of his back. The fire crackled and popped, throwing living shadows over her skin.

She squeezed and released in the perfect constricting rhythm, pressing her lips to the head of his cock as he pushed in and pulled out of her mouth.

Her other hand got busy with his balls, rolling them, lifting them, separating them with the length of one finger before she slipped that finger farther back to tease the rim of his ass. He liked that she had a backdoor obsession, but he liked even more the way she sucked cock.

He liked it so much that he had to give it up for fear that

he'd come in her mouth and then fall fast asleep. And he couldn't do that because he wanted to bury himself in her body and give her that mindless ride.

Leaning his weight on one hand, he reached down, took hold of his shaft, and pulled free from her lips, circling them with the head and dragging a trail of moisture from her mouth down her chest to her belly.

She whimpered beneath him, tucked her heels to her hips, held onto her ankles, and nudged him with her knees. She was hungry and impatient, and she smelled like sweet juicy grapefruit, and she was making him wish they had years to discover each other.

He moved to taste her, licking through her folds, circling her clit with the tip of his tongue. Her hips came off the ground that was hard beneath them. Her hands moved to grip the backs of his when he opened her, parting her plump flesh and sliding his tongue inside.

She writhed and moaned, crushed his hands with hers. "More, Jack. Please. I need more. I need you. Please, I need you inside of me now."

He needed her, too. He was shocked by how very much. He needed to feel her wet heat surrounding his cock, her muscles gripping him, milking him.

He needed to feel her belly on his, her breasts against his chest, her tongue sweeping along the length of his. He needed her arms holding him, her heels at his back urging him deeper inside.

He needed to kiss her, and so he did, pushing his cock into her pussy and his tongue into her mouth.

She welcomed him with her tongue that came to play, with her fingers that dug into his backside to pull him deep. Her hips pumped in a rhythm matching his, thrusting up when he thrust down.

It was an easy mating, and felt so good, so very good, and too right for words.

He didn't want to think about anything but his body and her body. He didn't want to think about hearts and minds and souls. This was purely physical, the way they were joined. It couldn't be anything else.

But he knew it was, and even knowing that didn't stop him from involving himself every way he could.

He cupped her head and continued to kiss her, his weight on his forearms, his chest brushing over her breasts, his cock sliding in and out from head to hilt, his balls slapping her ass.

She slipped a hand between their bodies, slid her fingers through her folds and opened them in a V around his erection. She toyed with her clit, tore her mouth from his, crying out as she shuddered around him.

He gave in. He couldn't hold out any longer. Not when he thought about the way she looked with his cock in her mouth. Or the way she took him into her ass as if nothing made her feel better.

She was wild, and she was chili pepper hot, and she milked him until he burned. He groaned, grunted, spilled himself into her, thrusting and driving until he was spent, until she was spent.

Neither one of them made a move to leave the other. And neither one of them spoke of their reluctance to lose this connection they'd found—a connection he doubted she was ready for any more than he was.

Chapter 23

The trek to the WRT transport station took two more days. Jack had hoped to make better time, to get there and be waiting when Gabriel arrived.

But he didn't know where he was going and had to rely on Jillian's nose. And Jillian seemed incapable of keeping her nose to the ground.

It wasn't anything in particular that she did, or anything at all that she said.

It was just the way she stopped their forward motion to backtrack several times. And the way she had to seek out a different trail when the one they were on reached a sudden dead end.

He wouldn't have thought much about it; he didn't expect her to know the island's every square inch. But watching her shake her head and hearing her mutter beneath her breath made him think she did know.

Made him think she'd been distracted rather than disoriented, that she'd lost her way because her head wasn't where it should be.

He couldn't blame her. His was hardly fastened on tight, or even at the right angle.

In fact, he'd been pretty screwy now for several days, and it

wasn't anything he could blame on the Mickey she'd slipped
him. He had no one to blame but himself.

Jillian at least had Joshua on her mind. Her worry for him
had to be brutal. Why Jack had egged her on about her son
and this Marco Chavero, he didn't know. The kid's paternity
wasn't his business. Neither were the child-rearing choices
Jillian made.

But he missed his son so much. Missed being a father so
much. He was projecting. He knew that.

He couldn't get back his time with Justin, and so he was
sticking his nose where it didn't belong because seeing the
parenting mistakes Jillian made—whether real or all in his
head—helped him feel a little better about his own.

And how fucked up was that?

They'd been moving uphill in their quest to get to the
other side of the mountain, and the journey had grown ardu-
ous, the ground damp, the plant life abundant, the humidity
cruel.

They spent very little of the daylight hours talking, using
their energy for the climb, and they made love silently when
they stopped for the night.

Jack didn't want to think about what it meant that they
couldn't find anything to say to each other—except what really
bothered him was that they weren't saying the things he knew
needed to be said.

He hadn't meant to tell her about Mandy. The words had
just slipped out. And he wasn't sure what it meant that doing
so hadn't hurt the way he'd expected, the way thinking of her
had hurt for so long.

He'd been the one to go after the women he'd been with
since she'd died. Sex had been on his terms—his terms being
that no woman was going to get to him ever again.

Not to his head. Not to his heart.

His body they could use and abuse at will, but he'd loved

well once, and he'd been loved well in return, and that would just have to do him for this lifetime.

Which is why it was a very good thing that he'd be here with Jillian for only a few hours more. He wouldn't have to test that particular theory, or rethink the stand he'd held fast for so long.

All he had to think about now was flying out of here and never looking back.

He glanced up ahead to where Jillian stood at the edge of the tree line, checking the clearing for any sign of Gabriel and her son. Jack was certain they should be here by now—especially since he and Jillian had been delayed by the cultists.

Though she hadn't told him how she was feeling, he'd been able to see the change in her as they'd drawn closer to the rendezvous point. She'd started to smile more often, subconsciously, he'd decided, since the emotion never did reach her eyes.

Her expression remained guarded, as if she didn't want to count too much on the end of their journey going smoother than had the rest of the trip, as if too much positive thinking was borrowing trouble.

As if she'd had enough trouble to last for the rest of her life.

Her son and his being here was the one thing Jack would regret never learning more about. No, regret wasn't the right word, he mused, stepping behind a tree as he lowered his zipper to take a leak. But it would've been nice to have his curiosity satisfied.

What could have possibly happened for her to think making a life in the jungle for her son was preferable to making one in Boston—even if she had cut all ties to her folks? Her father was a bastard, yes, but where was her mother in all of this?

And where was the boy's father?

He wanted to know. He knew it wasn't any of his business, but he wanted to know. He hadn't lived up to his promise to protect Justin, to teach him all the things a kid needed to know to go through life right.

Maybe if he could see Jillian's son, tell him one thing, like it wouldn't kill him to learn to do laundry, or to never draw on an inside straight, maybe if he could do that this experience wouldn't have been a waste.

And it wasn't a waste. He knew that. Sure, it would've been a lot better to have been asked to help out instead of kidnapped and forced, but he got why Jillian had done things her way.

She was the expert. She knew the lay of the land, the workings of the Sabastiano regime. She knew what it was going to take to get a pilot in the air. Yeah, a lot of things had gone way south, but those were things out of her control. He could hardly blame her for the raid on the camp or their being snagged by the cultists' guards.

In fact, he'd pretty much quit blaming her for anything at all, and knew flying out of here would be a bittersweet end to their jungle adventure.

He finished relieving himself, zipped up his fly, and glanced at Jillian as he grabbed his knapsack from where he'd dropped it. Only Jillian wasn't where she'd been standing. In fact, she wasn't anywhere around.

The skin of Jack's nape tingled. The hair on his arms stood on end. He knew she hadn't abandoned him; that would defeat her whole purpose of dragging him along.

More than likely she'd just stepped out of sight and knew that he knew to wait.

Except ten minutes later he was still waiting. And then twenty passed. At thirty, his antsy impatience had given way to panicked worry. But he had to keep his head on straight; hadn't he preached the same thing to her repeatedly?

Nothing had happened to her. Yes, he'd had his back turned. Yes, he'd been focused on himself. But this wasn't like

Mandy. He hadn't left Jillian to fend for herself while he stroked his own ego, working overtime, saving lives.

All he'd done was take a leak.

He fastened the strap of his backpack securely around his waist and moved to the tree line, keeping low to the ground as he scanned the clearing. The dock, the warehouse, the helicopter pad. All of it familiar in a weird déjà vu sort of way.

With his next breath he figured it out. *Son of a bitch*, he thought, shaking his head, his heart pounding. He knew exactly where he was.

He'd never seen a boat or a chopper when he'd flown over the point, but he'd seen the storage buildings there squatting along the bank.

That meant the Smithson compound was down the river, no more than six miles away.

If he hoofed it, he could be there in a matter of hours. Brief his crew. Put Smithson's bird in the air. Scour the jungle with infrared until he found her.

Then again, he could give her more time to show up before he took off and did something to cause her even more grief and bring down the same on himself.

He took cover behind a copse of trees, listening, waiting, hearing nothing but the sounds of insects and birds, the wind in the leaves, the water.

He heard nothing that sounded even remotely human. Nothing mechanical. No footsteps. No muttering. Nothing from Jillian or anyone who might have been anticipating her arrival and pounced.

Maybe she'd seen Gabriel and Josh from one of the warehouse windows and run down to the river's edge. Maybe she'd tripped on a tree root and taken a tumble. He really should wait. He needed to wait.

He'd been waiting forty minutes already.

He made his choice.

Chapter 24

Jillian had always wondered if she was capable of murder. She no longer did. If she'd had her machete, or one of the guns she so hated, or even a pencil with a sharp point, Carlos Sabastiano would be a dead man.

As it was, he was standing in front of her, gloating, looking so much like Gabriel's *Comandante* Mosquera she didn't know whether to cower or calm down. She did neither, standing her ground instead, chin up as she squarely met Carlos's steely gaze.

The Sabastiano *Policía* had taken over the WRT transport station, refusing to allow any incoming shipments until after the *Festival de los Santos* was done.

She didn't know how Gabriel's scouts had missed that particular tidbit, but it sure as hell would have come in handy when making plans to get Josh to the States.

Then she thought back to something Jack had said about a leak in the camp. Stomach churning, she thought, too, about her own denial that Gabriel would never whisper in his sleep, that Rosa would never share the team's secrets.

Jillian didn't want to think badly of Rosa any more than she wanted to think badly of Esteban or anyone else in the camp, but Esteban and his men had been the ones gathering intel. He had to be the one who dropped the ball.

Unless he hadn't dropped anything.

Unless he had a reason to keep what he'd learned to himself.

Unless he hadn't had to learn *anything* at all, but had known *everything* all along.

The only reason that came to mind was one she didn't want to think about. One that was standing in front of her, holding her captive, enjoying himself too much.

Carlos had been in power when she'd first come to San Torisco, and she now knew it was vodoun that kept him there. Not the religion that his dictatorship abhorred, or the village revelers he condemned as primitive, savage, a blight keeping progress from the island.

No, it was his own secret involvement, his own practicing of what he preached against that kept him king of all he surveyed.

But she hadn't been certain of that until seeing him again, here, out of his dictatorial element and at home in the costume of a vodoun priest.

She wondered if he'd been at the ceremony she and Jack had stumbled across that night. She wondered what he had planned for Jack. She wondered where Gabriel was, if Joshua was safe, or if Carlos's men had grabbed them, too.

Then she wondered if Carlos was going to kill her without admitting what he'd done to her that night. Or if shutting her up about the past—and his secret with her—was his only goal.

He was holding her in the WRT warehouse—the decidedly empty warehouse, thieving bastard—apparently waiting for the return of his men. After his private guards had tied her arms overhead, securing her wrists with a rope to a pulley, he'd ordered them to see to Jack.

They'd been gone at least an hour. There'd been no sign of them coming back. Her heart was in her throat, her stomach at her feet. She would not, would *not* let Carlos see her agony over the fate of her son, her best friend, and the man she knew that she loved.

She brushed damp hair out of her eyes with her upper arm, blowing to dry the strands clinging to her forehead. The strain on her neck and shoulders had gone from bothersome to brutal.

She had to convince Carlos to release her before she lost mobility and feeling. But she'd be damned if she'd kowtow to this man.

She shifted her weight, her soles scuffing against the concrete floor. "Whatever you hope to accomplish by holding me, it's not going to happen."

He pulled up a straight-back chair, the only piece of furniture in the place, and sat in front of her, his hands on his widespread thighs. "How can you be so sure, Miss Endicott, when you don't know what it is?"

She didn't have to know the details. She knew enough. "I know you. That means it's evil, criminal, and self-serving."

"Of course it's self-serving," he said with a caustic laugh, skipping over her other accusations and slumping back as if relaxed and watching a show. "Don't we all do what is self-serving? Isn't that part of the survival of the species? Seeing to our own needs first?"

When and where had he studied anthropology? Because the school needed its credentials revoked. "If you served your people, *all* of your people, the San Toriscans might have a higher rate of survival."

He pushed to his feet slowly. He was tall and well built, his carriage and his eyes intimidating, his physical strength unmistakable. Vileness radiated around him in waves.

He circled behind her, lingering close but out of sight. "You're overlooking natural selection," he said, his breath warm on her ear.

"No, *you're* overlooking the basic human rights of people

who expect leadership," she said, feeling the heat of his body along the length of hers, trying not to shiver and failing miserably.

She closed her eyes, swallowed the lump of dread in her throat. She would not give him that power over her. She would not allow him to win.

"What do you expect, Miss Endicott? Do you expect me to let you live?" he asked, running the backs of his fingers down the inside of her bare arms.

"I expect you to remove the *Policía* from the transport station and allow the WRT supplies to be brought in," she demanded, the strain on her muscles made worse when she flinched away from his touch. "And I expect you to let me, Jack, Gabriel, and Joshua go about our business and leave us the hell alone."

He moved his hands to her shoulders, cupping her neck, lifting her hair to his face and breathing in. "Let's talk about your son, Jillian. Let's talk about Joshua."

He wasn't subtle at all with his threat, and she inhaled sharply, telling herself he was nothing but a bully; this island, his playground; the villagers, the kids too unequipped to stand up for themselves.

She hated bullies. She hated this man more than any she'd encountered before. "No. Let's not."

"Then let's talk about your son's father," he said, before he kissed the back of her neck.

She didn't say a thing. She tried not to gag.

"Your team leader, Gabriel Corteze. He spends a lot of time with your son, doesn't he?" Carlos said, leaving her alone finally and returning to his seat.

She still didn't say a thing. She was still fighting the reflex to choke.

"There is no resemblance there," he told her as if she needed to know. "And my calculations tell me that their connection cannot be biological."

Drops of sweat rolled from the hollow of her throat into her cleavage. "Did you do them in your head, or use a calculator?"

He ignored her comment, leaning forward in the chair, his elbows on his knees, his laced hands close enough to touch her. He did, stroking his steepled index fingers from her knee up her thigh to her hip.

He stopped there, his gaze heated, his knuckles skating across the crotch of her pants. "I enjoyed very much having sex with you, Jillian. I'm quite certain you don't remember that you enjoyed me as well, but believe me when I say that you did."

"I don't believe anything you say." She stepped backward until nearly suspended, the movement tightening the tension on her arms.

She grimaced with the pain, a searing heat that burned hotter as she faced the man who had raped her. "Your lies are as self-serving as everything else about you."

"I served you well that night. Would you like me to tell you how?"

"I told you what I would like," she said, as panic set in. She did not want him to fill in the missing details of that night. She knew enough. Knew too much. The fact that this man had been inside her body . . .

"You're not looking well. I'm sorry the memory disturbs you. It's one that I recall with great pleasure." He got to his feet, stood in front of her, circled her waist with his very large hands, and pulled her close. "I often think of you when I'm with other women. I've never found another to be as firm as you are. As tight."

She spit in his face and he laughed. Then he slid his hand between her legs and fondled her through the fabric of her fatigues.

"I tasted you here." He squeezed the lips of her labia. "I sucked on you here." He squeezed her clit. "I entered you

with my fingers and my tongue. And with my very hard cock."
He straddled her thigh and rubbed his erection against her
until she wanted to scream.

He groaned. "Do you want to know what you said to me
when you came?"

"I did not come," she said, and ground her teeth together. If
she had, it had been the drink. She had been out of her mind.

He grabbed hold of her ass, his fingers digging between her
cheeks, separating them to find the spot he wanted. "You
asked me to bend you over and mount you from behind. You
begged me to slip into you here."

Not him. Never him.

She would never have asked that of him.

"You did come," he said, as he probed deeper, cupping her
sex with his other hand, his thumb fondling her clit. "I'm
going to make you come again."

"No." She shook her head, struggling as he played with her
through her pants. "Don't touch me. Get the hell away from
me now."

"Close your eyes, Jillian," he whispered into her ear, mas-
turbating against her leg while toying with her. "Think back
to that night. Remember how it felt to take me inside of you,
to close so tightly around me."

All she could think of was Jack.

He held her, violating her as she heated. She couldn't help it.
She remembered too well Jack's hands, Jack's mouth, Jack's cock
filling her everywhere. She didn't want this, but she did. This
was Jack. He was touching her, loving her, making her feel alive.

When she came, it was with Jack. When she cried, it was for
Jack. When she smiled, it was because of Jack. Jack, whom
she knew that she loved.

"Now," Carlos said, bringing her crashing down, reminding
her that it wasn't Jack here at all. "Let's talk about Joshua. *Our*
son."

Chapter 25

Jack could not get his mind off the fact that Jillian had a price on her head.

Did that mean "Wanted: Dead or Alive" posters had been stapled to tree trunks around the island?

That anyone who saw her could drag her into *Ciudad Torisco* for a bounty?

Is that what had happened?

The possibility scared the living hell out of him. She wasn't traveling in disguise, but as herself. Should she have worn camouflage? A costume?

Had she been too worried about her son to think about her own safety? Had she actually failed to factor her impending death sentence into their plans?

How could he have let that happen?

After she'd disappeared, his first instinct had not been to cut loose—which he'd have to examine later—but to head back the way they had come. To find the river, the cave, and the falls.

He didn't know what he thought that would accomplish except to help him get his bearings, but it had seemed right enough that he hadn't dismissed it out of hand.

From there he could track down the cultists' ceremonial grounds.

From there the remains of the guerrilla camp.

From there the fake prison.

From there the Cantina Mañana.

From there the Smithson Barracks.

Then he remembered that it had taken them nearly three days to get here. And that the *Festival de los Santos* would be starting in another four.

He didn't have time for a reversal, especially when Jillian had no reason now to backtrack. She'd pointedly told him the timing was critical for flying whatever it was out of here. He had to barge ahead.

Barging is what got him thinking about noise, and how he hadn't heard a thing when she'd gone missing.

And now he was sure she was missing and not just doing some sort of extra reconnoitering around the point because she'd been gone for almost an hour.

It didn't make sense that he hadn't heard a scream or a scuffle if she'd been dragged away into the jungle, down to the warehouses, or off the end of the dock.

Then again, he'd witnessed the San Toriscan way of doing things more than once. It didn't have to make sense.

Jillian had drugged him. She'd incinerated his clothes. He'd never seen either attack coming.

Had someone possessing even more spooky woo-woo savvy spirited her away? Hell, she could be tied up overhead in the trees while her captors waited for him to go.

He glanced up into the foliage. Oh, yeah. This was just great. Now all he and his overactive imagination were doing here was making things worse. Active. Productive. He wasn't being either. He needed to be both.

To think like an SG-5 operative rather than like their pilot. He'd been around Hank's Smithson Group long enough to know how this covert stuff worked.

His canteen was full. His socks were dry. He'd done more than enough waiting.

Though the vegetation grew too tall and too dense for him to get any directional help from the sun, there were no longer any shadows in the clearing past the tree line. The sun was directly overhead.

It was noonish, and coming up on the hottest and steamiest part of the day. He was looking at a six-hour hike to the Smithson camp, and plenty of light left to get him there as long as he got moving now.

All he had to do was hunker low to the ground, soldier his way through the jungle, keep the river in sight, and do it all without giving himself away.

This would have been a helluva good time to be Rambo, but being J. Jackson Briggs would just have to do.

Chapter 26

"I'm sorry to disappoint you," Jillian said, her elbows and ankles now tied to the chair in which Carlos had been sitting, "but Joshua is not your son."

He stood in front of her, one hand holding onto the rope dangling from the pulley. The trinkets at his ankles rattled when he crossed one foot over the other. She didn't raise her gaze any higher than that.

"Are you sure?" he asked her, though she didn't hear much of a question in his voice.

It held more a tone of gloating finality, and it started her stomach tingling.

"Or," he continued, "are you in denial because you've convinced yourself I disgust you?"

He did disgust her. She was especially disgusted by the sticky spot he'd left on her pant leg. "Convinced myself? Come closer. See if I don't vomit."

He laughed, the sound ominously low. "And earlier? I sensed nothing wrong with your stomach then. Or with any other part of your body."

It wasn't easy to shrug with her shoulders aching, but she did. And she grimaced, squinting as the sun dipped, sending a blinding shaft of light through the ceiling-high window into her eyes.

"There's no reason you should have sensed anything," she was very happy to tell him. "You weren't there. In fact, you didn't even exist. I self-servingly spent that time with someone else."

"I see," was all that he said.

She wondered if she had bruised his ego, or if he was too conceited to recognize an insult when it kicked him in the balls.

Then he asked, "With Jackson Briggs?"

She didn't respond. She was not going to let his goading get to her, even though her threat to throw up had not been an exaggeration.

She was sick with fear, with worry. The man had been hunting her down for days. Now he had found her. And she knew he hadn't even begun to do the worst he could do.

"Or were you with Marco Chavero?"

This time her gaze came up to lock with his, which was less malevolent than she'd expected, and mocking in a way she hadn't. It was as if he had a secret.

As if he wanted her to know that he did, but also wanted her to dig for it, beg for it, getting the same perverse pleasure out of making her squirm that he got out of making her come.

She thought back, looking for anything he could possibly know about that part of her past and finding nothing, finding no reason at all for him to have pulled Marco's name out of thin air.

Marco and his mother had left San Torisco when he was five years old. He hadn't been back since. He had, in fact, been gone so long, Jillian doubted anyone on the island remembered him at all.

Even if Carlos did, whatever he might've learned since had to have come from human interest stories in the media, the ones following up on her father's rescue of the indigent mother and son.

It was information easily accessed by anyone curious enough to look it up. But information that had no bearing on who Marco really was, what he meant to the island, what he meant to Carlos most of all.

He couldn't possibly have learned the truth, right?

Right?

"What are you doing down here at the point anyway?" she asked, fighting the urge to nervously swallow. She doubted the distraction would work but was going to give it her best shot.

She didn't want to reveal anything about Marco until she had a better sense of what Carlos knew. "Don't you have a goon squad to carry out your dirty work?"

When he still didn't respond, she added, "Or are you hoping to save yourself from paying out a reward by bringing me in yourself?"

"Actually," he began, shifting over in front of the light that was keeping her from seeing, "I'm feeling quite generous. So generous, in fact, that I believe I'll grant you a pardon."

He was done with wanting to kill her?

What? was her first response. *Whoa!* was her second. She'd never been formally charged or convicted of anything—hardly surprising—but now he was changing his mind?

That one threw her, but she remained silent, sensing anything she said would give him more of an upper hand than he already had by keeping her bound.

"Aren't you going to ask me what I've learned from you that has me willing to spare your life?"

"I'm more curious to hear what you've found out about Marco," she heard herself saying. "I haven't seen or spoken to him in years."

And, oh, but she wanted to slap the smirk off his face because he knew, he *knew* he had her.

Who in their right mind would ask about a childhood friend after hearing they weren't going to die?

She hadn't revealed anything to him, had she? Other than how much she hated him, and how joyous it had been to burst his paternity bubble.

That certainly wasn't the sort of truth she'd have thought would get him off her back. What was she missing here?

One of his dark brows hooked upward. The smile that followed chilled her. "I know that he grew up in your household. That you lived with him in South Florida. And I now know that you bore his child."

She snorted, hoping her derision convinced him more than it convinced her. She made a terrible actress, even if she had fooled Jack. "You're really fishing, aren't you? First you tell me Gabriel can't be my son's father. Then you contend that he's yours. Now you've decided he belongs to someone else?" Her panic pushed, and she curled her toes in her boots. "That's it? No other candidates in the running?"

"There's no one else it could be." He gripped the rope with both hands. It pulled taut, taking his weight when he leaned forward. "You and Jackson Briggs only recently became lovers. Your son is almost ten years old."

Ten years old . . .

"What?" she cackled, her throat closing fast. "You've been monitoring who I sleep with?"

He didn't say a word, and his silence cut a swath through her midsection like her machete slicing through grass. There was only one reason he would be questioning Joshua's paternity.

Oh, God.

He did know. He knew everything.

He waited for several seconds, letting the horror sink in, enjoying the way it invaded and spread, an aggressive cancer eating her alive. She felt the pain seize and crumble her bones.

Then he said, "It was important to me to know who you slept with following our tryst."

"It was rape," she croaked out. "Not a tryst."

"Since you returned to the States so soon after we were together, I had you followed."

Oh God. Oh God. "By a Peeping Tom?"

"I had to know if you became pregnant."

"Why?" she asked, her palms sweating, her lungs near collapsing, her heart attacking her chest. "You're a second-born son. Although it's a moot point, I thought you killed only firstborns of firstborns."

"It's not killing, Jillian." He came closer, letting go of the rope and walking to stand in front of her, large and looming, his trinkets rattling like bones. "It's a sacrifice required by our gods."

"*Your.* Not *our.* Now, since I've been pardoned, and since I'm not denying you visitation since my son is not yours, let me go." God, was she pulling this off? Was he buying into her chutzpah? "That way at least *I* can get back to serving your people."

"I can't do that. Since you have verified that he is not mine, then he belongs to Marco Chavero."

"So?" she asked, feeling as if bugs were in her hair and under her clothes, creepy, crawly, diseased. A nightmare like she'd never had before.

"Marco's father was my Uncle Romero. Though a bastard, a dogmatic loophole means he is the island's rightful ruler. A firstborn son. And Joshua is his firstborn."

"What are you saying?" She didn't know why she asked. She knew. She knew.

"I'm saying that though *you* are free to go, neither one of them can be allowed to live."

Chapter 27

Two hours into his trip—his chest heaving, his heart thudding, his eyes burning from the sting of dripping sweat—Jack heard voices. He careened to a stop, pressed his back tight to the closest tree trunk, and listened.

The chatter reminded him of that he'd heard between the Sabastiano *Policía* guards at the valley rim's outpost. It was conversational, though not particularly casual, as if those involved in the discussion didn't agree on the subject matter one hundred percent.

The speakers sounded just as young as had the others, but this time they spoke English with an island patois. A very good thing. Jack was too tired to translate. He wasn't even doing such a good job at picking up what he did understand.

Something about orders.

Something about captives.

Something about the others still out on patrol. That they should've been back a long time ago. That they thought themselves too good to follow rules.

Something about marksmanship skills.

Something about housecleaning.

Dissension in the ranks. That could only work in Jack's favor. He just had to figure out how.

With his pulse hammering him to find Jillian before the decision was made to clean up more than comrades, he willed himself invisible, pretended that it worked, then crouched close to the ground and crept slowly forward.

Before he caught sight of the voices' owners, the rear wall of a small hut came into view. It sat in a circular clearing, the back side abutting the tree line. A fire burned low in a pit thirty feet from the door.

Three Sabastiano guards—their skin dark, their heritage more Haitian than Hispanic—sat around the fire on plank benches like the ones that had been lined up in front of Gabriel's tent. A skillet like the one Rosa had cooked in was suspended over the flame.

Jack didn't know why he was walking down memory lane except that he wanted the good guys to win, and he wanted to string up the rest—starting with these three who, machine guns or not, deserved a round with bamboo and water until they told him where Jillian was.

They had to know where she was. They were too close to the WRT transport station not to. He'd bet money that they'd been assigned by Sabastiano as watchdogs in case Jillian showed up at the point.

It was her stomping ground, or at least one of the places anyone with reasoning skills and desperate to find her would think to keep an eye out. Not that this bunch had much in the way of smarts.

Why keep her here instead of hightailing it back to *Ciudad* Torisco and turning her over to the big guy who wanted her and was paying out the reward?

All they had to do was load her up on the horse they rode in on and ride out. It was a real camp, not a temporary shelter. They had to have a trouble-free way to access the place, and he doubted they'd walked here.

Since Smithson's crew wasn't finished with the construction

of the road, the patrols couldn't have used jeeps or Humvees™ to reach the site of their deployment. More than likely they'd come by boat.

Or by air . . .

The helicopter. It hadn't been there at the point.

Son of a bitch.

Gabriel had said it would be there. That Jack would see it when it was time to fly and not before. That the cargo would be there when he arrived, ready for loading.

And then it hit him.

Where were Gabriel and Joshua? Once Jack had realized Jillian was missing, the fate of the other two had dropped from his mind. He shouldn't have let that happen. They were easily in just as much danger.

Now he was really getting spooked. Was he going to disappear next?

He backed deeper into the jungle, giving the clearing a wide berth and creeping up slowly on the far side of the hut. The structure was built out of plywood sheets, and the front door was the only way out.

There were no windows. The gaps between the plywood provided the single room's ventilation. Jack snorted his disdain. Good to see Carlos Sabastiano treated his private police force as well as he treated his country's indigenous people.

But that same lack of quality did allow Jack to peek inside. He didn't see any additional guards or any more of Sabastiano's men. Neither did he see Jillian. He did, however, see Gabriel. And he saw Jillian's son.

Sitting on the dirt floor, the duo leaned against one of the hut's side walls. The boy had curled up against the man, his head on Gabriel's shoulder, his legs tucked up beneath him and angled into Gabriel's hip.

Gabriel's legs were stretched out, ankles crossed, his head back, one hand draped over his charge's knees. Though Jack knew in his gut they were not—no matter Jillian's refusal to admit Joshua's paternity—man and boy could physically pass for father and son.

But Gabriel's affection for the child was that of a good friend. A child he had taken responsibility for, whom he cared for, one he probably even loved, just not with the love Jack as a father had known for Justin.

He'd never bought into that bit about loving another kid like your own when he wasn't. It didn't work for Jack; it never had. It felt too much like lip service or the PC thing to say, when the truth for Jack was that it took more than saying something to make it so.

But this wasn't the time or the place for those thoughts, so he returned them to storage and dug for a way to get Gabriel's attention without startling Jillian's son, or alerting any of Sabastiano's men to his presence.

The latter shouldn't be that hard to do, considering the trio were still busy dissing their friends. Then again, one of them could get up at any minute to look in on the detainees. He needed to hurry.

A crowbar would go a long way toward splitting apart the plywood, but would make for a whole lotta noise and wouldn't do him a bit of good in a face-off with an M-16. He didn't have a crow bar anyway, so . . . moot point.

The best he could tell looking through the crack, a similar crack ran down the wall on the far side of Gabriel's head, four feet from the corner. Slipping a message of some sort through sounded like a plan. If he'd had pencil and paper, it would have sounded even better.

He backed way from the hut to the cover of the trees and hunkered inside a fall of downed limbs covered with ivy-like vines. He shoved his knapsack off to one side, cringing at the rattle of tins.

He knew the noise was muffled, but Jillian had drilled into him the need for silence, and if she'd been here, she'd have drilled him again. But she wasn't here, and he didn't know where she was, so he quietly concentrated on getting to Gabriel.

If he weren't afraid one of the guards would walk in and hear, or that a startled Joshua would bring them running, he would just whisper Gabriel's name. But since that option was out, he needed another.

Scratching a note on an ivy leaf might work, he mused, drying his forehead in the crook of his elbow. He could use the point of a stick, or snap one of the tongue depressors from his knapsack into a stylus of sorts.

And if the scratching didn't work, he could always write a note in blood. Or in peanut butter.

Peanut butter.

Who would ever expect to smell peanut butter in the jungle except for the man who'd stashed it in his emergency supplies? Even if he hated the stuff, Gabriel would have to think it strange to find it right beneath his nose.

The way his head and the crack between the sheets of the plywood were positioned, that's just about where a leaf smeared with the stuff and wedged through at the right height would end up.

Jack pulled out a tin and a tongue depressor, found a leaf with a stiff rib, and ate what peanut butter he didn't use for his message. Then he crept back to the hut to put his plan into action.

Joshua was the first one to stir. "I smell peanut butter."

Chapter 28

J ack peered through the crack, willing Gabriel to notice the same smell and to pick up the leaf from the floor.

He did, and he stood, turning to glance briefly at the wall, frowning as he said, "I do, too."

Good, man. Good. Now let's get this show on the road.

"I'm hungry." Joshua's words were a resigned whisper more than a complaint.

From where he was standing, Jack heard them clearly and wanted to give Jillian's son an "attaboy" for hanging in like a trooper. Instead, he kept his eye pressed to the crack and tried to catch Gabriel's gaze.

The other man squatted next to the boy, running his thumb over the crack where Jack had inserted the leaf, coming away with the remains of the peanut butter that had been scraped off on the wall.

He stuck the pad of his thumb in his mouth. And then he stilled, registering Jack's presence outside, shaking his head and chuckling under his breath.

Jack couldn't decide which was more clear: Gabriel's relief or his astonishment.

"What's so funny?" Joshua asked.

Gabriel pivoted on the balls of his feet to look at the boy. "You stay here. Don't move until I get back. Understand?"

"Where are you going?"

"To see about getting you something to eat." Hands on his knees, Gabriel pushed up to stand, staring at Jack as he added, "Wait for me exactly where you are."

Jack got the message, though he did move several steps back. He felt safer beneath the cover of trees than out in the open—especially when the guards who'd gone AWOL could return at any time.

He heard Gabriel call out to his captors, heard what sounded like orders to stay put, heard the argument that followed and Gabriel basically telling them to stuff it; he didn't care what they said.

He was going to answer the call of nature and look for something to eat. He made a whole lot of noise on his trip to the rear of the hut, blowing off their threats and demands that he stop.

The minute he came into view, Jack lifted one hand. Gabriel saw the signal, stacked his fists and swung his arms as if batting at a ball, and then motioned that company was coming.

Jack scanned the ground, grabbed up a club-like length of wood, slipped past the tree line to the hut, and pressed his back to the side wall. Then he waited, his chest pounding as if he'd just stepped on a land mine and could do nothing but anticipate the blow.

"Yeah, yeah. Get over it," Gabriel was saying, passing the corner where Jack stood and continuing into the trees. He lowered his zipper, turned his head to the side to watch the guard's approach peripherally.

He nodded when it was time.

Pulling in a deep breath, Jack counted the seconds until the guard passed the corner of the hut, and then he swung.

Hard.

The club slammed across the man's back and sent him to the ground. He groaned as he crumpled, the air whooshing out of his lungs.

And then Gabriel was there, silencing him with a mouthful of leaves, ridding him of his weapons, dragging him into the brush. A couple of pounding blows, and he left him there unconscious, rejoining Jack.

They agreed with crude sign language not to say a word, silently communicating their joy at finding each other and Joshua safe, their shared concern over Jillian's fate, and their need to get to her now.

Jack held up two fingers, signaling that he'd seen only two more guards on site, then gestured that they get ready to repeat the process. Gabriel nodded. Jack grabbed up the club and returned to the side of the hut.

His back pressed to the plywood wall, he crossed his fingers that number two went down with even less effort. Less than five minutes later, he got his wish.

It was when the third arrived following a longer wait that Jack sensed trouble. Gabriel didn't give him the same sign. Instead, he turned and lifted his hands shoulder high in surrender.

He didn't look Jack's way at all, but gave all of his attention to the approaching guard. "Joshua, you okay?"

Son of a bitch.

Jack kept his gaze trained on Gabriel, waiting for word on what to do, not wanting to jump the gun and give himself away to the guard or to Jillian's son. Whenever it was time, he needed the element of surprise on his side, and to steer the boy clear of danger.

"I told him I was hungry," Joshua said, his voice remarkably steady. "That you were only looking for something for me to eat."

Gabriel kept his hands raised and nodded briskly. "That's good, Josh. And that's all I'm doing."

"It is not all you are doing." The guard's voice wasn't half as calm as Joshua's. "Where are the others? What have you done with them?"

"I haven't done a thing," Gabriel insisted. He lowered one of his hands, ran his palm over his forehead to wipe it free of sweat, then his index finger across his neck as if doing the same.

The guard had a knife to the boy's throat.

That's all the gesture could mean.

Jack was already sweating, but his perspiration now reeked of fear. Joshua's life was in Gabriel's hands, the guard's fate in Jack's.

That's how it had to be. That was the only way it could be if they expected to get out of this with Jillian's son still alive. He signed to Gabriel that he'd take on the bigger man, that Gabe would take care of the boy.

Gabriel backed another step away from the clearing and into the thick growth of trees. "The boy's hungry. Let me pull up these roots I found and get him fed."

"No. You will return to the hut immediately. We will feed you when we decide it is time."

"I can wait. The boy can't." Another step. Then one more. "There's no need to punish him. You can punish me, but first let me get him something to eat."

Jack saw the toe of Joshua's boot. Then the toe of the guard's.

"Make it quick," the guard said, his gaze on Gabriel, his entire body coming into Jack's line of sight.

"I will. But let the boy go," Gabriel said. "He's not going anywhere, and he's no threat. All you're doing with that knife is scaring him. Just drop it."

He cut his gaze to Jack at the end, and Jack took his cue. He came out swinging, the club whomping down onto the guard's shoulder. His scream wasn't loud enough to cover up the sound of bones shattering beneath the blow.

Gabriel lunged for the boy. Jack went for the knife. He sliced through the strap holding the machine gun to the downed man's back, stepping away as the guard writhed face-first on the ground.

"Who's that?" he heard Joshua ask.

Gabriel answered, "Remember the man your mother brought back to camp? The one she took with her to pick up supplies?"

"When we got raided, you mean?"

"He's the one," Gabriel said, gathering all of the weapons as Jack took Joshua by the shoulder and led him away from the scene. No ten-year-old needed to see any more of what had happened than he already had.

As behind them Gabriel hauled off the third guard, leaving him with his friends and silencing him as he had the others, Jack offered the boy his hand. "My name is Jackson Briggs."

"I'm Josh. Joshua Endicott." He pumped Jack's fingers. "Where's my mom?"

Jack lifted his gaze, met Gabriel's as he returned, and let him answer. "Jack and I need to talk about your mom."

The boy's eyes were the same whiskey gold as Jillian's. He looked from man to man. "Is she all right?"

Jack cleared his throat. He wasn't going to lie, but he didn't know how much of the truth to tell. He settled for, "The last time I saw her she was just fine. And she was looking forward to hooking back up with you."

Again the look, back and forth, back and forth. "So where is she now?"

Gabriel stepped in. "You got any more of that peanut butter, Jack? I wasn't kidding when I said Joshua here was hungry."

"Sure thing."

Joshua sighed. "I'm always hungry."

"That's because you're ten years old."

"Not for another week. Right now I'm still nine," he said from behind Jack as they headed for the dead, ivy-covered branches and his knapsack.

Once the boy was settled cross-legged in Jack's hiding place, a tin of peanut butter in one hand, a tongue depressor in the other, Jack and Gabriel walked several yards away toward the clearing side of the hut.

"What happened to Jillian?" were the first words out of Gabriel's mouth.

"I don't know. I lost her."

"What?" Gabriel yelled, then lowered his voice. "What do you mean, you lost her?"

"We were at the point," Jack said, waiting for his own pounding from the other man's fists. When it didn't come, he continued.

"She was standing at the tree line, looking around, obviously looking for you and Josh. But you weren't there. And then . . ." he shrugged, ". . . she wasn't there."

"Where'd she go?" Gabriel asked, his fury as palpable as his worry.

Jack felt like a fool. He should have paid attention. He should have kept his eyes on her at all times. That's what Gabriel, as a friend, would've done.

That's what Jack, who loved her, should've done.

The realization of how much he did crushed the air from his lungs and nearly broke him. Another minute passed before he found his voice.

"I was taking a leak. She was there when I stepped behind the tree. She was gone when I stepped back. I figured she'd moved down the way a bit, seeing if she could find a clue as to where you might be."

"And so you did what?" Gabriel asked, a brow arched in menace.

"I waited." Thinking that's what Jillian would have wanted instead of thinking for himself. "Probably too long. When I did start looking around, I realized that I'd flown over the point dozens of times. I was headed for the Smithson compound to put the chopper up and search. That's how I ended up here."

"Goddammit," Gabriel said, the word followed by several that were much more choice. "I know where she is."

Jack's heart exploded. "What?"

"The guards. They were talking earlier. It didn't register at the time because I thought she was still with you."

"What? What? Where is she?"

"There were five guards here when we arrived. The two who grabbed us from the docks went back to set up a patrol around one of the warehouses. That has to be where they're keeping her."

The gears in Jack's mind began to whir. He pointed to his right. "The Smithson compound is another four hours or so downriver. Gather up anything around here you might need, and head that way with the boy."

"No," Gabriel said sharply, his gaze fierce. "You head that way with the boy. I'm going back for Jillian."

"I'll go back for Jillian." Jack stepped in front of him. This point was nonnegotiable. "Josh knows you. He doesn't know me. My luck, he'd cut out and I'd have to hunt him down, too."

"Then we'll all go. We can't get into the compound anyway, remember? Not with Carlos's patrols circling it 24/7."

"Yeah. You can. But you have to come up from the river." Jack explained the back door that had been put in as an emergency measure after the crew learned exactly what it meant to work in San Torisco.

He didn't even wait for Gabriel's response. "You make sure Joshua is safe. I'm going back for Jillian."

Chapter 29

Jillian had never in her life been so glad to see the Sabastiano *Policía* arrive anywhere.

After Carlos's pronouncement that both Marco and Joshua were going to die, she'd gone numb. She'd had no choice. It was a measure of self-protection.

The only way she knew to stay strong.

If she'd let herself dwell on what Carlos had said, her mind would've shut down. She couldn't let that happen. Her mind was going to get her out of here. With her body bound and her emotions strained, her ability to analyze her situation, calmly, logically, was all that she had.

Her head told her that things were not right in Carlos's world, were wrong in a very bad way. He'd left her tied to the chair, sitting in the center of the warehouse, and gone to huddle near the door with his men.

Something was up. Something that made him uneasy.

Something his men deemed important enough to warrant an interruption. What was bad for him could only be good for her, right?

She bowed her head, chin to her chest, and closed her eyes, struggling to hear any of what they were saying. But the distance between here and there was too far, their voices pitched too low.

All she could do was pray that Jack had found Gabriel and her son, that the three of them were safe, that whatever the guards were saying, it had nothing to do with the men she loved. Gabriel, Joshua . . . and Jack.

Because she did love Jack. She didn't know when it had happened, when she had fallen; they'd had so little time. But the man that he was . . . she sighed.

She wanted hours and weeks and years to know him better. It would take that long to learn all she wanted to know about him. It would take longer to see where this love could go. That's what she wanted. Time with Jack. Time with Jack and her son away from this place.

Carlos cut into her thoughts, issuing orders, his words clipped, his tone low and harsh. Jillian sensed his displeasure with his men and what they had told him, sensed their fear at bringing the news.

He closed the door, said nothing to her, moved to the corner of the room where for the first time she noticed a small wooden chest. He picked it up reverently and carried it closer, placing it on the floor five feet away.

From here she could see the crude scenes etched into the panels, scenes that looked a lot like the art found on cave walls, but were clearly religious in nature—an observation Carlos confirmed when he bowed his head and kneeled in front of it, splaying his hands over the top.

She held her breath, staring at his dark hair, at his shoulders held tense, at the exaggerated rise and fall of his chest as he breathed; and listened to the rattle of the trinkets around his elbows and wrists when he sat back and lifted the lid.

She had no idea what he was doing, but there was no way she was going to ask. The man in front of her was no one she knew. He was in a trance, but he wasn't calm or relaxed as she'd expect from someone dazed. He was wound up, taut, intense and frighteningly so.

He pulled a small leather pouch from the chest and poured a line of dark powder around himself, making a circle on the warehouse floor. Then he exchanged the pouch for a pipe, lighting the tobacco packed in the bowl—tobacco she was certain was laced with an hallucinogen.

She was right. The pungent smoke stung her nose, caused her eyes to water. She couldn't imagine the effect it was having on him, but expected any moment he'd look up at her with glowing eyes, horns piercing his forehead.

He laid the pipe at his knees, reached into the chest a third time and withdrew a larger pouch. She heard the contents clatter, and her stomach fell when he poured the small animal bones into his palm.

He worried them from right to left, rocking back and forth as he rubbed them with his fingers, cupping his hands together and bringing them to his mouth, blowing and chanting words she did not understand.

She didn't have to.

As she looked on, his erection thickened and rose like a tent pole in his pants.

She wanted to laugh at the absolute absurdity of it all— What had Jack said? That laughter was the best medicine?— but feared her hysteria would draw his attention before she'd figured a way to free a hand or a foot.

Either would work to incapacitate him if she could get enough swing room to hit him where it would hurt. Was sex the only thing he had on his mind? The only way he had of getting what he wanted?

He returned the bones to their pouch, dumped the tobacco onto the floor and tucked the pipe away, carried the chest back to the corner.

Then he came to stand in front of her, the Carlos of before.

"Unfortunately, my dear Jillian, I'm not going to be able to release you as promised."

"I never thought you would." If he wasn't going to talk about what had just happened, she sure wasn't going to bring it up. "Your promises are only one of the multitude of things about you that are worthless."

"I would enjoy nothing more than to spend the day matching wits with you, I get so little of that," he said, his voice gentle, a soft smile on his startlingly handsome face. "But I'm afraid duty calls."

Jillian snorted. "She must have the wrong number."

"Not at all. She's the one, in fact, who has insisted it is time for me to plant my seed," he said without prelude, tugging off his shirt, reaching for the waistband of his pants. "To produce the fruit that will yield a child."

"Why?" she asked, struggling with her bonds, struggling equally to keep a straight face when her insides were screaming in panic. "So you can kill him?"

"My firstborn has already been destroyed." His pants came down. He kicked them aside.

She looked away, toward the door, her mind racing with the admission he'd just made. He'd had his own child killed?

"The child you conceive will be my second."

"You're out of luck." She squinted as the door opened a crack, as a shadow appeared and took shape. "I can't conceive," she told him, shaking her chair, swaying back on two legs. "I took care of that after the birth of my son. He's the only child I'll have."

"Oh, but you will conceive. It is ordained that you do so. That we marry the old ways of my beliefs with yours, which embrace current times."

He kicked up the dust of the powder he'd poured out, made a bowl of his hands to catch what he could of the cloud and breathed it in.

"The gods will make it happen." He raised his hands overhead, let the remaining powder rain down. He opened his mouth and swallowed all that he caught.

Jillian nearly gagged. Hurry. She had to hurry.

"Our child will rule San Torisco with the understanding of both of our worlds," he said, taking a step toward her. "He will have the understanding and patience I do not, and your generosity of heart."

"No. He won't," Jack called once he'd pushed open the door. He waited for Jillian to crash her chair backward.

Then he raised the machine gun he carried and opened fire.

Chapter 30

It took forever to get Jillian untied from the chair and out of the warehouse that reeked of dope and death. Jack had just killed the dictator of San Torisco.

He didn't even want to think about the trouble he was in. All he wanted to think about was getting Jillian out of this place and reunited with her son.

Until that happened, nothing else—including the fate he'd just sealed for himself—would matter.

"We won't tell anyone," she was muttering, flinging aside the ropes he'd cut from her wrists. "No one has to know it was you."

"They'll know," he said. He wasn't going to deny what he'd done. He had no need to broadcast it, but he wouldn't pin it on anyone else if pressed.

"Who knows you're here?" she asked, still flat on her back, her head up as she watched him work through the ropes at her feet. "Where did you get the gun? Is Joshua safe? Gabriel?"

"They're both safe. They both know I'm here. I got the gun from one of the three guards holding them," he told her, returning the knife he'd taken off the same downed man to its scabbard, leaving out the part about that man holding a knife on her son.

"But they're fine, right? They're not injured? You're not hiding anything from me?" Freed, she scrambled to her feet, rubbed the circulation back into her wrists. "Jack. Please. Don't hide anything from me."

"I'm not hiding anything. I promise." He grabbed hold of her upper arm and propelled her toward the wide-open door. "Let's go."

"Wait," she said, and pulled up. "The guards outside. Were they there?"

"They were. Now they're in the river." That's all he was going to say. "Let's go."

Still she didn't move. At least not in the direction he was desperate for her to go. Instead, she stared at him, her chin quivering, her eyes welling with tears. And then she launched herself into his arms.

He held her as she shuddered, her sobs so tight inside her chest he wondered how she could breathe. Her hands clawed at his back, as if he wasn't close enough, as if she needed more than he was giving her.

He wanted to give her everything, but he couldn't do that here. And he couldn't do it now that he'd just fucked up the rest of his life.

The only thing that gave him hope was that he worked for Hank Smithson, and Hank had made a whole lot of trouble disappear over the years for his men.

Jack had never asked him for that kind of favor. It might be time to do so now, because he couldn't imagine letting this woman go, never seeing her again, never holding her, touching her . . .

"I can't believe I was so careless," Jillian said, sighing as she stepped away, wiping her hands over her eyes before snagging her whip, machete, and backpack from the ground.

You weren't the only one, sister.

"I wasn't thinking," she went on. "If I hadn't been so consumed with getting to Joshua, I would've realized the helicopter wasn't here! That should've been my number-one clue that something was wrong. That Carlos knew we were coming."

"Don't be thinking about anything but getting out of here." They needed to get moving.

It would be getting dark sooner rather than later, and that six-hour hike he'd never finished before was still going to take six hours. Only when they hit the Smithson compound would the pressure on his chest begin to ease.

Her eyes grew sad. "I think you were right."

"About what?" Jack nodded toward the door, pushed it shut once they were through and latched the bar, locking Carlos's body inside.

"That we had a leak in the camp." She shivered, ran her hands up and down her arms.

He knew she wasn't cold; it was about a billion degrees out here. But he did know she was scared, and worried, and focusing too much on things she couldn't change.

"I don't know if it was Rosa," she said. "Or if it was Esteban. I hate to think it was either one, but they were the closest to Gabriel."

"Meaning they'd know all his plans."

She nodded, stared off toward the helicopter pad, and huffed.

He followed the direction of her gaze, kicking his own ass while she kicked hers. "You're being too hard on yourself. I didn't notice it wasn't here either until I was an hour downriver."

"Downriver?" she asked, scurrying to catch up as he jumped from the dock to the bank. "Where? Where did you go?"

He made a sweeping gesture before he ducked inside the tree line. He doubted there was anyone around. "Once I saw the warehouses, I figured out where I was. I'd started off for the Smithson compound. I ran across Gabriel and your son at a Sabastiano outpost about two hours away."

"They're not here? With you?"

He shook his head, watching her glance around frantically.

"Where are they now?"

"I sent them to the compound. It's safer for them to wait there than have your family reunion here." He didn't mean to be short with her, and didn't know what had happened to his patience.

Unless he was still reeling from killing one man and probably two others.

The guards at the warehouse he'd taken out one at a time, shoving their bodies into the water after they'd crumpled to the ground from the butt of his gun to their heads.

"You should have gone with them," Jillian snapped back. "I can't believe you didn't go."

"I wanted to make sure you were found," he bit off, wondering why this trek didn't rate the silence of the other, thinking it should, but doubting it would when Jillian had so much to say.

"Then *you* should've taken Joshua and let Gabriel search," she said, her voice growing shrill. "You know how important it was, how vital it was, how vital it *is* to get Joshua out of here."

"No. I didn't know," he said, her words reverberating until he was too dizzy to go on. He stopped. In the middle of the path they were making, he stopped, stunned, his ears ringing from the rush of blood.

She took several more steps, noticed he was no longer beside her, and turned. "You didn't know what?"

He looked at her. Unbelievable. Freakin' unbelievable. She was still in denial that he needed to know. And worse. That he deserved to know.

"You told me you had vital cargo. This is the first time you've told me that cargo is your son."

She dropped her gaze to the ground, lifted it a moment later to stare into the deepening gloom. "I couldn't let you in on our plans. If you'd been caught or if you'd escaped, I couldn't chance you telling anyone else."

He bristled. "Thanks for the vote of confidence."

This time she looked at him, her repentant expression feeling like too little too late. "I didn't know you then, Jack. Besides, it wouldn't have mattered."

"Oh, it matters."

"I don't get it." She frowned, the motion emphasizing her scar. "How would knowing about Joshua any earlier have made a difference?"

He wanted to laugh. Goddamn, but he wanted to laugh. What a joke. This whole endeavor. What a miserable fucking joke. "Because I could've saved you a whole lot of trouble by telling you then that I won't fly a kid."

Chapter 31

He wouldn't fly? *He wouldn't fly?* "What are you talking about, you won't fly?"

"I won't fly your son," he said, and started walking again, brushing past her without another word and disappearing into the trees.

"You're a pilot," she called after him. Then she ran after him, tripping on a stubborn root that wouldn't get out of her way. "That's what you do."

He spared her a brief backward glance before he trudged on. "I fly equipment. I fly a finite number of grown men who've seen more danger than I might possibly put them in. I don't ferry passengers. Ever."

"Wait," she called, and because he didn't she had to process what he'd said on the run. "Are you saying you don't want to fly Joshua because you think you'll put him in danger?"

"Not because I think, because I *will*."

The man had been out in the sun too long. There was no other explanation for his insanity. "How do you know that? How can you possibly know that?"

"Look around, jungle girl." He waved one arm in a sweeping gesture. "Machine guns. Magic dust. Murder. And then there's that bit about a price on your head. Don't those say danger to you?"

She slowed, falling a couple of feet and then a couple of yards behind. Her boots were splattered with Carlos's blood. It was probably dried in her hair.

She couldn't remember a time when the risks that came with the life she'd chosen hadn't weighed on her like a yoke. But the last week, the last few days, realizing what it meant to have made the same choices for her son, to have put him under the same burden . . .

She was his provider, his tutor, his counselor. She was his mother, for God's sake. She'd schooled him herself, had seen to his health, had made certain he understood the good work they were doing here, that he took pride in his part, that he enjoyed it.

She'd wanted him with her so she would know he was cared for, safe, happy, and loved. God, she was the only parent Joshua knew, and for nearly a week now she'd been a fugitive, one of San Torisco's "most wanted."

What in the world was wrong with her? Why had she ever thought giving her son this life was smart?

Gabriel would have taken care of him, of course, if anything had happened to her, but what would her son think when he was older, when he learned how selfishly she'd acted, how irresponsible she'd been?

And Jack thought *he* was going to put Joshua in danger? The thought made her want to laugh.

"Jillian?"

He'd walked back to where she was still standing, where she was shaking, her arms crossed over her middle for fear she'd fall apart.

"Before he died," she began, clearing the thickness from her throat. "Before he died, before you got there, Carlos gave me a pardon."

"What? When?" he asked, hitching at the straps of his knapsack. "In the warehouse?"

She nodded. "When he was . . . holding me."

"Just like that. On a whim."

"Yep." Though she wasn't sure she'd have called it a whim. Calculating seemed a much better descriptor of the way Carlos had worked.

"He can do that?"

"He's the dictator." Or he *had been* the dictator—a realization that had yet to sink in. He had too many minions on the island for her to accept that his reign was done, that he couldn't get to her from beyond the grave. "He can do anything he wants."

"What did he say?"

"About pardoning me? That all he was looking for was information."

"Wait a minute." Jack shook his head as if doing so would dislodge something that made sense. "You didn't break any laws, you didn't hurt his feelings, he wasn't trying to get you out of the way. He put a price on your head because he wanted to ask you a question?"

She nodded.

"Did he? Ask you?"

She nodded again.

"And you answered?"

One more time. "Yes, though not willingly."

Jack's nostrils flared, his eyes grew flinty. "He forced you?"

"More like . . . tricked me. He didn't use physical force. He didn't . . . hurt me," she lied, because it was easier than telling him about the way he had touched her, the way she hadn't fought back.

"Hurt doesn't have to be physical, Jillian." Jack came closer, his expression softer now, almost warm, his voice kind. "I saw what he was trying to do."

She didn't want kind. It was too easy to collapse under kind. She needed him to be firm, even harsh, to force her to keep steady, to go on. She could do it on her own; she always had. But leaning on Jack . . .

Was it so bad that he made things easier? "I'm fine. I have to be. I can't fall apart until Joshua is safe. After that?" She shrugged. Would there even be an after? "Then I can fall all I want."

"Joshua is safe. He's with Gabriel. I told them how to get past the guards and into the compound." Jack reached up, brushed stray curls from her forehead, looked at her hair instead of into her eyes. "Nothing is going to happen to you or your son."

She would've felt better if he'd said that to her face instead of to the top of her head. "That's not good enough. Carlos may be dead, but he had time to tell his men what he'd learned."

"The men guarding the warehouse? Trust me. They're no longer a problem."

"Not now, no. But they could've radioed any number of others."

"And told them what?"

"About Joshua's father."

"Marco, right?" he asked, and then he stepped away, his gaze slamming into hers so hard she felt the air leave her lungs.

"Jack—"

"It's not Carlos, is it? Jillian? Could Joshua have been Carlos's son? Is that what he thought?"

"Yes," she admitted, and when he spun away added, "Jack, wait. It's not what you're thinking."

"How do you know that?" he spit out. "You have no idea what I'm thinking."

"Yes. I do." The calmness of her voice surprised her. Even her trembling hands had steadied. "It's what I would be thinking if what had happened with Carlos had been anything but rape."

"He raped you? He *raped* you?" he asked a second time, as if the emphasis made the word real. "*Son of a bitch.* It was that ceremony, wasn't it? The one like we saw. The one you'd seen before."

She nodded.

"You could've told me." He moved toward her, stopped, backed away, returned, his expression tortured, torn. "You could've told me."

"Why?" She watched him pace, wondering what he was thinking, not sure that she wanted to know. "Telling you wouldn't have changed a thing."

"I know. I know." He stopped, laced his hands on top of his head, his chest heaving with his frustration. "But I swear, if we were close enough I'd kill him again."

That made her smile. "It wouldn't do any good."

"It would do me a whole lotta good."

"Thank you, Jack," she said softly.

He shook his head. "Don't thank me until I figure where to go from here."

Easy one. "We go to the Smithson compound."

"I mean once we're there. I can't fly Smithson's Chinook alone. I need a copilot and a flight engineer."

"Then you gather your men."

He shook his head.

"Is that a no? No, you won't gather them?"

He dropped his knapsack to the ground, braced one hand against a tree, rubbed the exhaustion from his eyes with the other. "There's got to be another way. We can use one of the crew boats. Head to Aruba or Curacao."

"What are you saying?" A boat? He wasn't making any sense. "A boat is too slow. Joshua's still in danger."

"I told you. He's fine. And he'd be a lot safer on the water than he'd be in the air."

"He's not fine, Jack! And he's not safe! If Carlos got word to his men, they'll be looking for Joshua to kill him!"

Chapter 32

Kill Joshua? What the hell?

"What are you talking about?" If this adventure took one more twisted turn, he'd swear he was dreaming the whole thing, not living through the nightmare.

Jillian shook her head, or so he thought until he realized it was her whole body shaking, and that she wasn't refusing to answer, but could barely stand up.

She'd been kidnapped and held hostage, then nearly raped by the same man for the second time in her life. Then she'd wound up close enough to a hail of gunfire to feel the heat.

He hadn't given her time to recover from any of that before he'd had her on the move. It was a wonder she was standing at all.

Especially since she hadn't slept in days. He knew that because he'd been wide awake at night with her, watching her toss and turn. Now he knew the why of her insomnia.

His didn't even begin to compare.

"Listen, Jillian. We're not going anywhere until you tell me what's going on. All of it, understand? There's no way that my knowing can make things any worse."

"It's about Joshua's father," she said, her voice cold and flat as if her fear had all rattled away, leaving her lifeless and numb.

He wanted her alive, vibrant, snapping at him to keep his voice down and his feet moving. Anything but this. "We've been over that already."

"Not this part." She took a deep breath, tossed her backpack to the ground next to his. "Marco's father was Romero Sabastiano. Carlos's uncle."

"And Carlos is dictator because Romero's son was one of those kids who was killed," he said, his brain whirring, kicking into high gear.

If he was understanding what she was saying . . .

The obvious hit him hard enough to bruise. "Marco Chavero. He was Romero's firstborn."

Jillian nodded, rubbed her hands up and down her arms, stepped closer to the tree he'd been leaning against as if finding it safer to talk from the shadows. "Marguerite was a servant in Romero's house. They had an affair. Marco was the result."

"And that's why she took him and ran."

"The fact that he's illegitimate doesn't matter. He's still Romero's firstborn son."

And Joshua was his. Whoa.

"That's why Marco's never come back to the island." *Why you've taken full responsibility for Joshua. Why you've not wanted to let him out of your sight.* He couldn't think of anything more to say.

"Carlos had me followed for weeks to see whether or not I'd conceived," she went on to explain. "I went to Florida not long after. Marguerite had died, and I spent some time there with Marco."

"And Carlos couldn't be sure whether he or Marco had fathered your child."

"He couldn't be. But I could."

Smart girl. "You had Joshua's paternity tested?"

"Marcos and Carlos are related," she said as she nodded. "But Marguerite's medical records proved she was his paternal grandmother."

Jack took a few seconds to digest what he could. "This was the information Carlos wanted."

"I had no idea he knew about Marco. I just couldn't stand that he thought Joshua might be his." She buried her face in her hands and dropped to sit cross-legged on the ground. "I told him he wasn't. He didn't even ask. I just told him. Straight out."

He hunkered down beside her. "Jillian—"

She cut him off with her eyes, her gaze slicing sharply into his, desperate, begging. "I need you to take Joshua out of here, Jack. Please."

"We'll get him out of here. I promise," he said, swearing to keep this one no matter what.

"I'm so scared." The shakes returned, set in to stay. Her skin appeared bone white. "I don't think anything has ever scared me this much."

"Shh. It'll be okay," he said, cupping his hand beneath her chin, lifting her face, looking into her eyes . . . and then kissing her. Kissing her. Right.

As if that was going to make anything better with all she'd been through today. But then she calmed and came close, and he decided to stay.

He loved the way she felt, the way she gave when he asked, yielded when he pressed. But it was so much more than that. She made him feel like he was the only man on earth, the one she needed the way she needed air.

And then she curled into his body, her mouth moving to his ear where she whispered, "Make love to me, Jack. Please?"

He was a goner. He couldn't think of anything he wanted more. Hell, he could hardly think of anything when she fit him so well, her lips nuzzling beneath his ear, her teeth nipping, her fingers pinching the skin in the hollow of his throat, but he did.

He thought about how much they needed rest. Then about how night would be their best traveling time. Still, a few hours spent here before leaving wouldn't hurt, and they'd still get to the Smithson compound by dawn.

And, really.

With the way she was crawling all over him, slipping her hands beneath his T-shirt, tugging at the hair in the middle of his chest, and oh, mama, tweaking both of his nipples and straddling his lap, there wasn't a chance in hell he was going to say no.

He could feel the warmth of her sex on his thigh, and his cock responded, swelling in record time and to record size. She took note of that. He felt her smile against his jaw where her lips were pressed.

He was glad she could smile. She needed to smile. It was the next best thing to laughter, and a whole lot safer right now. Besides, he had the rest of his life to listen to her laugh . . .

"Hey, you," she whispered against the shell of his ear. "Where'd you go?"

"I'm here. Right here." The rest of his life? "This won't be any fun if I'm anywhere else."

"If you're here, then why are you suddenly sitting there like a stump? This won't be any fun if you sit there like a stump."

He was not about to tell her that he'd been thinking about forever when he didn't need to be thinking of anything but now. "That's no stump, sister. That's a pole, if not a pole and a half."

"Hmm." The sound came up from her throat and wasn't quite steady. "This pole business is something I may have to see to believe."

She was tired, jittery, and he wanted her. But he didn't want to make the rest of the night harder to get through than had been the day. He dug through the lust that was choking him to find his voice.

"I'll give you a look-see on one condition," he said, holding onto her hips while scooting closer to the tree.

"What's that?" she asked, as he leaned against the trunk, taking her with him, her weight on his chest.

"You do this because it's what you want. And that you don't want it because having me touch you will make you forget about him."

He couldn't see all of her face. The branches and vines and leaves above masked most of the light from the moon. But he could see her eyes, and the scar that bisected her brow when she frowned.

"I may play war games, Jack. But I don't play sex games. I've had three lovers in my life. Three." She held up the same number of fingers. "That includes you. Just because I love sex the way that I do doesn't mean I get off with every Tom, Dick, and Carlos Sabastiano I meet. I also have to love the man I'm with."

His heart beat the air right out of his lungs. "Did you just say that you loved me?"

She nodded, the motion sending ringlets of hair bouncing around her face. "I did. And I know it's too soon. And I know it's complicated. And I know it doesn't make any sense. And I don't expect you to feel the same."

Did he? Feel the same? "Well, I—"

"Shh." She put two fingers over his lips. "Don't say anything. Especially something you may not mean. I just wanted you to know." She took her hand away, placed her lips near the corner of his, added softly, "It's important to me that you know."

He turned his head and kissed her, sweet pecking kisses that kept him from having to speak. He didn't want to open his mouth and tell her that, because he'd loved Mandy, making love had given him a high he'd never reached while flying—and that he'd felt the same blown-away rush when on the cave floor with her.

It was a whole lot less complicated just to kiss her. He didn't have to think about what he was doing or what it meant. Or deal with the fact that he already knew. All he had to do was open his mouth over hers.

He did that, and he cupped the back of her neck to hold her where he wanted her, sitting up straight when she insisted on stripping off his shirt before she stripped out of hers.

He could still smell the soap they'd used when they'd bathed in the pool at the falls. It was there with the smell of their sweat mingled with the heat of the jungle. Yeah, they both needed a bath, but he had never cared about anything less. The only thing he cared about was getting naked all the way.

Jillian reached back and unhooked her bra, but he stopped her from peeling off the cups. He was hungry and greedy, taking the weight of her breasts in his palms, teasing the swells above the silky fabric with the flat of his tongue.

She nearly melted him with her whimper. "Do you remember when we were sitting in front of Gabriel's tent and you touched me like that?"

His mouth was busy, so he answered with a nod.

"You made me wet my pants. In a good way, of course," she said, and chuckled. "Sitting there without squirming was one of the hardest things I've ever done."

"You should have squirmed," he said before he dipped a tongue beneath the bra's fabric and rolled her nipple around. "I like it when you squirm."

"I like it when you do what you're doing." She groaned, the sound caught tightly in her chest. "You have a wonderful mouth."

"And you have wonderfully tasty tits." What he wouldn't give for a mattress and a week of this. "You make me think of candy."

She tossed her head back. "You make me think of sex. All. Of. The. Time."

He drew her nipple into his mouth, sucking her through the

silk, holding her with the barest edges of his teeth and flicking back and forth with the tip of his tongue.

"Can I come now? Please?"

His laughter rattled deep in his chest. "You can come as many times as you'd like."

"I'd like a dozen orgasms at least."

"We might need a bed with clean sheets and soft pillows for that."

"And handcuffs. Don't forget the handcuffs."

"I like it," he said, and got rid of her bra that was suddenly in his way, pressing her breasts together, deepening her cleavage. "You have very fuckable tits. Tasty and fuckable."

"Find me that bed, and I'll let you fuck me any way you want."

"I've always been a pretty vanilla guy."

"There's nothing wrong with vanilla that chocolate sauce can't make better."

"So now you want handcuffs *and* food?"

"I want it all, Jack. I want everything."

"Demanding wench, aren't you?"

"Do you think you can keep up?"

"What I think is that I like you on top."

Chapter 33

"Oh, it's like that, is it?" She loved the way he made her feel as if nothing beyond this moment mattered when they both knew the world outside was waiting. "You're going to just sit there on your ass?"

"I think so." He buried his face between her breasts, his breath warm, his lips warmer. "It'll save us both the hassle of digging dirt and dead leaves out of all sorts of crevices later."

Yeah. This jungle-sex business was for the birds—and the monkeys. She liked her tent and her cot and her really thick sleeping bag. She'd like that bed even better. "Worse than a day at the beach, isn't it?"

With a sigh, Jack let go of her breasts, moving his attention to her belt and zipper and dipping a finger inside her panties to tease. "I'm trying to remember if I've ever had sex on the beach."

She gave a quick shudder, spared a quick thought for West Palm Beach, then grabbed his T-shirt and shook it out to spread on the ground beneath them. "Trust me. Between the sand and the salt left behind? It's not all it's cracked up to be."

"Heh." He got up and out of the rest of his clothes. "You said crack."

She did the same—and went breathless at the sight of his jutting cock. "How old are you again?"

"Thirty-nine. You?"

"Oh, years, years younger." She reached out, held him in her hands. His shaft, his balls, the slitted tip of his glans. He was thick, unyielding, so incredibly soft, and she went ripe with waiting.

He shuddered, cleared his throat. "Jillian? How old?"

She was ancient, knowing everything. She was a child, not knowing all that she should. "Old enough."

"For what?"

"For this," she said, kneeling to wrap her lips around him.

He filled her mouth, and she loved the way that he did, his shaft solid and warm, the skin taut, the head of his cock so resilient when she pressed it with her tongue.

She ringed her fingers around him and squeezed, released, teasing the tip of his bulbous head, lapping at the moisture that quickly beaded there.

He groaned, his hands in her hair as if he wanted to drive to the back of her throat, to make love to her mouth as thoroughly as he had the rest of her body.

She moved her hands to his hips and set the rhythm, starting slowly, rocking, her lips forming a tight "O" as she pulled him in and pushed him out, as she tempted him to pick up the pace.

He took the hint, adjusting his stance and spreading his legs, his fingers flexing against her scalp. And then he began to pump, the motion of his hips increasing. He thrust harder as she sucked, then groaned, the sound a strangled cry of near pain.

"Jillian, wait, stop—"

But she didn't stop. She kept on. She wanted this for him as much as she wanted it for herself.

She palmed the bottom side of his shaft, thumbing at the ridge and the seam that split it, licking at him with the flat of her tongue until he came.

His semen bathed her mouth; she swallowed and stayed with him, waiting for him to finish, to pull free and step back. He did, and then she smoothed out his T-shirt, showed him where to sit, and climbed back into his lap.

He gave her a weakly arched brow. "Again?"

She laughed softly. "I'll give you time to recharge."

"Does that include a nap?"

"Sure. Take all the time you need." She parted her thighs and settled her sex over his groin. "Just let me see your hands before you drift off."

He flopped both onto her knees as if spent beyond repair. If she hadn't been having so much fun—God, when was the last time she'd had fun?—she would've laughed at his puny theatrics.

Instead, she curled her fingers over his wrists and coaxed his hands higher. The pads of his index fingers were rough; she shivered with the friction, sliding them up and down through her folds the way she liked.

She lifted her chin, closed her eyes, played with herself until nothing existed but sensation . . . the feel of Jack's thighs flexing beneath her, the hair cradling his penis catching on hers when he moved, his penis stirring, bobbing against her.

She pinched her distended clit with his fingers, rubbed the hard bud where her nerves tingled like static electricity shocks. She was as erect in her own way as he had been, and the feel of his hands made her shudder.

When he took over, she shuddered anew, opening when he probed her center, tightening when he pushed two fingers inside, squirming when he added a third.

His cock knocked against her bottom, tapping her there between the front and the back. She slid one hand between her legs, reached down between his to heft the weight of his balls and roll them in her palm.

But then Jack bent forward to lick at her nipples, and she had to let him go. She was helpless to do anything but enjoy.

She braced her hands on his knees and let her arms hold her weight, leaning back and giving him all the access he could need.

He parted her pussy's lips with one hand and held his cock with the other, stroking up and down, circling her entrance, circling her clit, spreading her moisture as he would paint, coating her, priming her, taking her beyond ready and into bliss.

That's where she was when he pushed into her. She felt that first breach, the ridge of his head catching there and holding. He gave her no more than that. And then he stilled.

She groaned. "You are a mean man, Jackson Briggs. A very mean man."

"What I am is hard. Very hard. And this one's going to last for awhile . . ." he paused, adding, ". . . if you're still wanting that dozen."

At that, her eyes came open. She sat up slowly, impaling herself completely on his cock. She ground against him, squirmed, decided to hold out just because he made waiting so much fun.

But then she met his searching gaze. Whatever was happening behind his eyes was enough to make her catch her breath, to worry that her loving him had been too much.

She didn't want her love to hurt. She didn't want him to fear he was damaging her.

So she placed her palms on his shoulders and told him wordlessly—with her body, with her heart—that she was fine. And that he was the one who had made her so.

Chapter 34

They started for the Smithson compound three hours later. Jack knew that Jillian needed more sleep, but she *had* slept. She'd even snored, very softly, and he would never tell. He didn't want her to obsess about having let down her guard. Besides, he'd enjoyed listening to her.

A lot.

He'd insisted they dress before dozing. He liked the idea of spending that downtime with her naked body wrapped like Christmas paper all over his.

But the idea was not the same as the reality. And the reality was that they were in San Torisco, not the Garden of Eden.

The other reality was that he never should've dropped his pants to begin with.

Not that he hadn't had a helluva good time waving his flag in the breeze. The good Lord and Joe Bob knew that he had. But as much as he cared for Jillian, he didn't know how smart it was to be loving her, or have her loving him.

This thing. It felt like a whole lot more than a convenience, or a way to pass the time. It felt real and alive and so much . . . bigger than what he'd shared with Mandy that he didn't know what to do, because he sure couldn't let it go.

Bigger. That didn't mean better. It did mean more consuming—which made a lot of sense, considering he and Jillian had been living on top of one another for days. And that was why he should've kept his pants on.

This wasn't the jungle adventure Jillian had deemed it. They were running for their lives, and adding sex to the mix of turbulent emotions was a very bad idea. Messy now. Hard to clean up later. All the questions and repercussions and uncertainties.

Yeah. A very bad idea.

"Hey, flyboy," she called from where she was walking behind him. "Answer me a question."

Why was he pretty sure giving her an answer would up the heat of the water he was treading here? He wanted to get to the Smithson compound, find Gabriel and Joshua, then check in with the site foreman and see about borrowing a few armed men and a crew boat for the day.

He'd endure Jillian's wrath. He would not purposefully put her son in more danger. Still, he slowed. He didn't want her to lag too far back. It was dark, and they were sharing the flashlight from her pack to conserve the batteries in the other.

They were also walking closer to the river than he felt comfortable doing, but the moon was bright, and with the reflection off the water they could see farther than they could with the single beam alone.

He heard her on his heels and said, "Ask away. Just make it quick and make it quiet. We don't want to attract any unwanted guests."

She slapped his rump, moved to his side. "That first day in the jungle? When I whipped you to the ground? Remember?"

Like he would ever forget. Like he'd ever want to. "My best Charlie Brown impression ever. What about it?"

"What were you thinking?"

He frowned. "When?"

"When you flipped me over. There was something in your eyes."

At least she hadn't noticed the something in his pants. "I was thinking that I was one sick mother for wanting to make it with a nun."

She sighed heavily in response.

He'd expected sarcasm at least, if not a dressing-down over the truth of his colors. "That's it? A sigh? No recommendation of counseling? No admonition that I get my ass to confession ASAP?"

This time she snorted, dodging the same low-hanging branch he'd already ducked. "Who am I to rain on anyone's fantasy? I'm the one living in the jungle, trying to make a difference in the world."

"Trust me," he said, wondering if there was a difference between giving up and giving in, and which one she was on the verge of doing. "Mine was a perversion. At least yours is a noble cause."

"Ah, but what foolish price noble?" she muttered more to herself than to him.

She'd been strong for so long and through so many things. A few hours more, and she could fall into as many pieces as she liked. He'd pick her up at the same time he picked up himself.

He reached for her hand and squeezed. "Your son is going to be fine. You're going to be fine. The island I'm not so sure about, but you've done what you can do. What else is there?"

She didn't answer, she just held on until she had to sidle behind him and scramble around a pile of dead timber. Once she had her feet beneath her again, she asked, "Can I ask you something else?"

Her exhaustion was getting to her. He couldn't think of any other reason she was asking his permission for anything. "If I say no, are you going to ask me anyway?"

"Yes."

That was better. "Shoot."

"If Gabriel and I had managed to get into the Smithson

camp and explained everything to you there, would you have taken Joshua out?"

"By air? No." The beam from his flashlight picked up foamy bubbles at the water's edge. "But we're on an island. We don't need air. We've got water."

"He would have stopped you, you know. Carlos. His men. They would've searched your boat. To see if I was onboard. Or if you'd stashed Joshua below deck."

He didn't say anything. He was planning to use a boat now. Carlos was dead. But his men didn't know it. They would still be looking for Jillian and her son.

"Jack?"

"Jill?"

"I told you about Marco and Joshua. I told you about my father and Marguerite. I told you about Carlos and what he did to me."

He knew what was next. She'd bared all, and now had decided it was his turn. He supposed he should be grateful. At least she hadn't tossed their physical relationship into his face with the rest of her bargaining chips.

"Are you ever going to tell me why you won't fly my son out of here?"

"Can't," he insisted, his jaw taut and aching as he fought not to say more. "Not won't."

She ignored him. "You told me you don't want to put him in danger. He's already in danger. I don't buy it."

So it came down to this. Number three out of twenty questions, and she'd cut straight to his heart.

He swallowed hard. It was dark. They were alone. By this time tomorrow, she'd be nothing but another notch on his past.

What would it hurt to dredge up the two graves he'd dug so long ago? If the pain got too bad, he could crawl in and pull the blanket of dirt over his head.

"The accident that killed my wife?" He waited, tested the

sore spot, found it tender but bearable and went on. "My son died in the same one."

Her breath hitched. "You had a son?"

"Justin," he said, focusing on the flashlight beam bouncing on the ground. "He was five."

"I didn't know." Her voice was soft, a barely discernible whisper.

"There's no reason you would have. I don't talk about him to anyone. I've never even told Hank."

"Hank? Smithson?"

He nodded. "I'm sure he knows. Hank knows everything about everyone working for him. But he never learned about it from me."

"Jack, why didn't you say something before?"

"I just told you. I don't talk about it to anyone." Though he was talking about it now, wasn't he? Sap. Such a sap. But now that the floodgates were open . . .

He budged his pack higher on his shoulder. "Justin and Mandy died because I didn't keep them safe. I didn't protect them. If I'd been home like I should've been, the accident wouldn't have happened."

"You weren't there?"

He said nothing.

"But you're blaming yourself anyway?"

He really didn't like her tone. "I took an extra shift I didn't have to take. I flew Life Flight. Aeromedical rescue. Mandy had wanted me to spend the day running errands. It was Christmas. We had a lot of shopping to do and had promised Justin we'd get a tree."

He hadn't thought of the details in so long. How angry Mandy had been when he'd called her that morning to tell her he wasn't coming home. How he'd blown her off, knowing she'd calm down by the time he showed up that night.

How he'd planned to get some sleep, take them out for pancakes and a trip to the mall to see Santa. How, instead, his first call had been to the scene of the accident that had killed them.

"I put them in danger by being in the air instead of on the ground." He'd made the same choice his father had, to put work before family—a choice that had cost two innocent lives instead of his own.

His stomach clenched around the bile stirring there. "I'm not going to make the same mistake with your son."

"You were working. It was an accident. Jack, listen to what you're saying. If you'd been behind the wheel, you wouldn't have saved them. You'd have died, too."

He wasn't going to talk about this anymore.

"They didn't die because you were in the air." She was frantic, insistent, as angry as Mandy would have been. "They died because some asshole ran into them."

He wasn't going to talk about this anymore.

"Goddammit, Jack. Your flying is *not* going to put Joshua in danger. It will take him out of more danger than any kid should ever be in. You know that." She hounded him, ruthless as she pushed, nearly breathless with alarm. "Tell me you know that."

He wasn't going to talk about this anymore.

And now he didn't have to.

He looked up after rounding an outcropping of rocks, and the Smithson compound came into view.

Chapter 35

Jillian had been to the Smithson compound only a handful of times during the construction crew's year on the island. She'd never made it past the perimeter fencing, though not for lack of desperation and dogged persistence, so she had no idea what she'd find inside.

What she was seeing now was nothing like she had ever imagined she'd find behind the gates.

The place was in ruins. Pure chaos. Equipment smoldering. Vehicles overturned atop puddles of oil and gasoline. Pots and pans from the mess hall strewn around the yard with the mattresses and bed frames from the barracks. Tool belts, hard hats, safety glasses, stacks of rebar—all scattered. It was a disaster.

And it chilled her to the bone.

Sabastiano's men had finally justified the search and destroy they'd been champing like leashed pit bulls to do. She didn't believe the attack had been precipitated by his body being discovered. They hadn't had time to do that and come back here and do this.

No, this had happened before Jack had rescued her at the warehouse. Someone had given the guards the go-ahead.

The only reason that made sense was that the Sabastiano *Policía* had learned of Jack's kidnapping and had lifted the prohibition banning any search of the Smithson compound for clues to her whereabouts.

That intelligence had to have been leaked by the same informant whose betrayal had sent Carlos to ambush Jillian, Jack, and Gabriel at the point. And to think that the leak had come from her camp, from someone she'd trusted, from someone she swore she'd see pay . . .

Her stomach rolled, the acid inside churning as she tried to absorb the impact—and the implications—of what she was seeing. How were any of them going to get off the island now, and where were Gabriel and her son? Had they arrived before this had happened? Had they escaped along with the others? Had they even made it here at all?

"Jack?" she finally found her voice to ask, staring at the horrific scene and the detritus spread inside the fence like so much trash in a landfill.

He was as speechless as she was. All he did was shake his head, one hand scraping at his scraggly beard. She looked at him standing there, his broad shoulders hunched, his clothes stained and torn, his arms scratched, bruised, and speckled with bug bites.

His expression was too weary for words. She'd exhausted all other outlets and had been counting on him since day one to save her son. He hadn't been her last resort. He'd been her *only* resort, and she'd been asking too much, thinking only of Joshua and herself.

If she hadn't drugged Jack and stolen him away, he would've been here with the others. He would've escaped and been on his way home. But now he was stuck just like she was. On an island with no way to get off.

And a very dead dictator rotting on the floor of a warehouse.

Could she have screwed up any more lives? "I'm so sorry, Jack. I'm so, so sorry."

"Don't be." He kicked at a coffee mug and started walking around, picking up a screwdriver and tucking it into his pocket, as if salvaging the one tool could possibly make a difference.

She brought her hands up, tented them over her face but didn't say a word. She just watched him and waited and listened, hoping he wasn't hating her.

"The boats weren't at the dock. And I don't see anything indicating anyone got hurt heading out. Insurance will cover the property damage. We'll be up and running again soon." He paused, adding, "Just not here."

He was right, and that truth made her so very sad. No one would come to San Torisco after this. The road would never be finished. The WRT services would be suspended indefinitely—if not forever. Any progress that had been made would never be fully realized.

But that wasn't what mattered.

"I don't mean about this. I mean, I *am* sorry about this, of course I am." She didn't want to cry, but tears welled. Sorrow. Exhaustion. Fear. She felt it all. She ached with it all. "But I'm more sorry for everything I've done to you."

He turned to face her, stared down, not hating her at all, but looking at her as if she were his port in the storm, his island; as if they were the only two people on earth. She wanted to scream; it felt like they were. Her son, her best friend, they were nowhere to be found.

The damage . . . it was apocalyptic.

"I love you, Jack," she said, her vision blurred. "I know you don't want to hear that, but it's true and it's real. I've hurt you, and I'm sorry. But I'm not sorry that what I did brought you into my life."

She watched his throat work as he swallowed, watched the redness of emotion rim his eyes. His hand came up and he cupped her jaw, swiping his thumb over her cheek. "I'm not sorry either. And you've gotta know that I—"

"Hey, Mom! Jack!"

What?

Jillian spun at the sound of Joshua's voice. Her heart in her throat, she launched into a flat-out run as he came toward her from across the yard.

Gabriel was there behind him, heading away from the helicopter pad and Jack's big Chinook, its props mangled like scrap metal and scraping the ground.

Joshua was almost as tall as she was, but that didn't stop her from picking him up and twirling him around and around like a carousel gone wild until he yelped, "Mom! I can't breathe!"

Laughing, crying, laughing, she stopped and set him down, turning to Gabriel, who snatched her up, spiraling her in even more and faster circles until she yelped, "Stop! You're making me dizzy."

Once she was steady on her feet, her happy tears making it impossible to see, she pulled her son close, listening to his chatter—*Had he been this tall last time I saw him? Had his voice really been this deep?*—while Gabriel and Jack shook hands, then backslapped and punched each other silly.

Men will always be men, she mused with good humor, her heart light for the first time in days as she realized how very much she loved the two, but finally rolling her eyes and interrupting to ask, "Gabriel, what happened? Where have you and Joshua been?"

"Here, believe it or not." He looked and sounded as exhausted as she felt. But she also sensed his relief. "We came in the way Jack told us to and found the place just like you're seeing it."

"We hid inside the big helicopter," Joshua added. "We knew you'd come to look for us, so we watched for you and waited." He turned and looked up at Jack. "Do you have any more peanut butter?"

Jack laughed, tousled the boy's hair. "My pack's by the gate. Have at it."

"Hey, Mom," Joshua said, ducking away, a ball of energy as he scampered toward the knapsack. "Get Jack to tell you about how he used peanut butter to break me and Gabriel out of prison."

She turned to Jack, surprised at how easy it was to breathe, how calm she felt, how hopeful. Surprised most of all by her ability to feel anything besides discomfiting unease when they were still standing smack in harm's way. "Peanut butter?"

He snorted, and though his eyes teased, a palpable worry still weighed him down. "I have talents you can't even imagine."

She ached with wanting to touch him, to hold him, to massage the strain from his shoulders. "You mean there's more than I've already seen?"

Gabriel cleared his throat, his gaze clicking from one to the other. "I think I'll see if I can find something besides peanut butter."

"We should all start looking for something besides peanut butter," Jack said to both of them, saving Jillian from trying to find her voice or a way to explain to her friend things best kept for later.

Jack went on saving her. "Even if the Chinook weren't a wreck, the crew's gone. The boats are gone, too. Forget using any of the trucks or jeeps. We're going to have to hoof it, and we need supplies. *Ciudad* Torisco's our best bet, and that's what? Twenty miles?"

"Those boots you're wearing?" Gabriel glanced down at Jack's feet. "WRT issue, my friend. They're made for walking. We're all four good to go. Though you might want to tie yours back up."

Jack crouched down, paused, picked up what looked to be

the chewed butt of a cigar. He brought it to his nose and sniffed. Then he smiled. And then he laughed.

"Son of a bitch," he crowed, the others looking on.

"What?" Jillian finally asked as Gabriel hovered, and Joshua came running back.

"God bless America, we're getting out of here."

Chapter 36

The cigar saved his life. Well, Jillian Endicott saved his life, but the cigar got him off the island.

Truth be told, the moment he picked it up, he forgot all about being unable to fly and remembered what it meant to save lives, that thing he'd been born to do.

He hadn't had a lot of time to let Jillian's outburst sink in before they'd reached the compound. He did know the things she'd said, well, it was a lot of the stuff he'd felt stirring over the years, stuff that lived at a gut-deep level he didn't dig around in too much.

He'd found it a whole lot easier to wallow than to mine for the truth.

He'd grown comfortable carrying the blame. It fit. It covered a lot of sins. Without it, he'd have to face the meaningless loss of his wife and son. If there was more to their deaths, if there was a *reason* they'd died and if *he* was that reason, he'd thought the loss would be easier.

Still debilitating, just not so insane.

But it would never be easier, and taking the blame had made it all about him instead of about the family he'd loved. Jillian was right. An accident was an accident. That's why it wasn't called a *purpose*. It could have happened anytime, and even if he was there.

He'd known when he spotted the butt of the Montecristo Corona Grande that Hank had been to the compound since the kidnapping. He'd no doubt flown down to the job site *because* of the kidnapping, hoping his being there for the search would somehow help.

With Jack out of commission, Hank would have put Gideon Martel in the cockpit for the flight. Gideon had flown Navy Seahawks and knew his way around a multithreat environment. And with both men having evacuated with the rest of the crew and the compound trashed, Jack was certain no one had found Hank's Bell.

He hurried across the yard, yelling at the others to stay put and praying that the lift gate controls were still in one piece, that the cables and underground power source were intact and fully operational.

The years Hank had spent at the helm of the Smithson Group working under both law enforcement and governmental radar meant he took precautions that were nothing less than ambitious. Jack had never been so thankful.

Hank made sure his engineering crews—as well as his covert operatives—would never be left behind, or forced to endure insufferable conditions. He valued the hours they put in, did what he could to minimize their risks, and this time he'd made sure Jack had a way out.

For the project in San Torisco, and because of the unstable military dictatorship, Hank had given the crew orders to construct an underground hangar, and Jack knew that's where he'd find Hank's personal craft.

He bounded onto the overturned concrete steps and through the job site's office trailer's sagging door, slamming his palm against the big black button next to the row of electrical sockets and switches on the wall.

When he heard the grating mechanical roar of gears grinding, it was hard not to drop to his knees and wail like a baby. Instead, he headed back to watch with the others, chuckling at Joshua's awed "Wow!"

The ground beneath their feet began to shake, the dirt hopping and popping on top of the two metal plates opening in the center of the compound to reveal the cavernous hangar below. Once the hydraulics locked the hinges, securing the doors, the lift began to rise.

As the helicopter's props came into view, Gabriel tossed back his head and laughed like a hyena. Joshua whooped and hollered, jumping up and down.

Jillian stumbled back in disbelief, a hand clamped over her mouth, her eyes as wide as her son's. And then she began to cry, huge racking sobs filled with so much relief, Jack felt like a god.

He grabbed her by the waist and kissed her senseless in front of everyone, then let her go and said, "Gimme thirty for the preflight check, one stop halfway to refuel, and we'll be home."

Chapter 37

Hank Smithson and two of his SG-5 operatives, Gideon Martel and Simon Baptiste, were waiting on the roof of the four-star hotel when Jack set down the bird seven hours and fifteen hundred kilometers later.

Simon he could understand being there. More than likely he'd been in the States anyway. But how Hank and Gideon had made tracks to Miami so quickly after evacuating by boat with the engineering crew . . .

What the hell was he thinking? Jack didn't know half of how Hank Smithson managed what he did.

Once the prop quit stirring up debris from the roof's surface and Jack gave the okay to approach, the two members of the Smithson Group hurried forward, greeting him with big grins and slaps on the back, before helping Jillian, her son, and Gabriel disembark.

Jack made quick introductions, hanging back as Hank started toward him, feeling a hard jolt at seeing Jillian walk away and sag affectionately against Gabriel's body on their way to the elevator doors.

Jack was supposed to be at her side, be the one she turned to, leaned on, couldn't live without. Yeah, he'd gotten her kid out of San Torisco in one piece. He'd saved her life and Gabriel's, too.

But she hadn't said a word to him since they'd left the island. Nothing. Nada. Zilch.

He'd kissed her there in the compound, done his ground and cockpit check, signaled for the others to board, and lifted off once they were safely strapped in.

Using the frequency that would put him in touch with SG-5's Manhattan ops center, he'd radioed to let the boys know he was coming home.

Jillian and her son had slept in the seats behind his and Gabriel's, and the other man had remained silent for most of the flight. Jack had done the same, focusing on getting to the States, thinking about what he wanted to say to Jillian now that the jungle was behind them.

Unfortunately, seven hours hadn't been enough time to find the right words—which probably went a long way in explaining why he was standing here by himself waiting to talk to Hank.

But then, she'd told him she loved him, and he hadn't said a thing.

"I never could figure why you gave up flying and went to living on the road." Hank rocked back on the heels of his boots and gestured with the cigar stub he held between two fingers, watching as Jack went through his postflight check. "Not enough room in a duffel bag for all the things a man needs."

Jack shrugged. He'd done okay during those years. They'd gotten him to where he was now, and he couldn't complain about that.

Hank stuck the cigar in the corner of his mouth, rolled it to the other, his hands in his pockets tugging his jacket down. "Can't fit a humidor."

Jack smiled. He didn't smoke.

"There ain't room enough for a good racehorse."

Jack wasn't much for the track.

"And forget packing in a woman and all the things she's gonna need to spruce herself up."

Jack thought of Jillian living in a tent and trekking through the jungle without a complaint. He wondered if she was already in a tub, waiting for a pedicure. He wondered about the scent of her soap, if after a bath her skin would still smell like the heat of the sun.

"A model copter might fit, but I don't see that satisfying that thing you've got for being in the sky."

Jack squinted into the setting sun. It kept him from having to see the face of the man who'd done everything for him. Who'd picked him up when he wasn't going anywhere and given him direction.

The idea of disappointing him . . .

"I killed a man," he said, pulling in a deep breath, tucking his clipboard under his arm. "A first for me. I spent a lot of years saving lives. I should feel something for taking one."

"It'll set in, boy," Hank told him directly. "We'll be here when it does."

The older man considered him a part of the Smithson Group. Jack liked that. "I'm not as worried about what I did as I am about who I did it to. That's not going to sit well with a lot of people."

"It'll sit just fine with the folks who matter, and the few who'll ever know. You exterminated an evil, Jackson. And that's all we're going to say about that."

The cigar came back out of his mouth. He used it to make his point. "What I want to know is if you're done with the duffel bag and ready to bunk in a place of your own."

"Why? You have some swamp land to sell me?" They were in Florida, after all.

"I'd figure that girl of yours might be ready for a cooler climate. And I've been thinking for awhile of downsizing the Sarasota farm. Lots of room there for a boy to run."

Jack stared in the direction Jillian had gone. Was she his girl? It was time to find out.

Chapter 38

"I have a surprise for you," Jack said, closing the door to the opulent suite behind them.

And boy, if opulent hadn't been the word of the day, Jillian mused, realizing it described everything about the hotel where she'd been the last twenty-four or so hours.

After a full twelve spent sleeping in the penthouse, Jillian and her son, along with Gabriel, had been treated to an incredible day, starting with a room-service feast—all courtesy of Hank Smithson.

She couldn't remember coffee ever tasting so good, or maple syrup making such a mess. But then when was the last time she'd had a food fight with her son? Or laughed until her ribs ached?

Haircuts and new clothes followed for all of them. The guys then spent the afternoon poolside, while she'd settled in at the spa to do something about her feet. She didn't know what had become of Jack.

She hadn't seen him since they'd landed last night. She'd hoped he would join them for breakfast, or at least stop by and say hi. But it wasn't until Hank arrived later in the day that she heard a thing.

Before Jack's boss whisked Gabriel and Joshua off to

Kissimmee for a minor league baseball game, he told her to be ready for dinner at eight. Minutes after the three had gone, the first-floor boutique sent up a dozen dresses and shoes in her size. She played fashionista the rest of the day.

Jack had arrived right on time, wearing a tux and carrying a single red rose. He'd been quiet, reserved, kissing her softly, then taking her downstairs to a private table on the restaurant's terrace.

Their evening had been the stuff of pure romance. Candlelight. Violins. Sunset and sea breeze. Champagne that tickled her nose and made her laugh. Prawns that melted on her tongue and made her moan.

It was beautiful, but it wasn't her, and it made her long for the jungle.

She'd been out of civilized circulation for so long, she didn't know if she wanted to jump through the necessary hoops to fit in. As long as she had her tub and the occasional pedicure, she was happy living in khaki.

And her idea of romantic? She didn't think anything could match the night she'd spent on the cave floor with Jack. No clothes. No trappings. A fire for warmth. Food to sate their hunger, water for their thirst.

Peanut butter would do her as long as she could eat it with Jack. And tonight, with her son taken care of, the man she loved was the only thing on her mind.

"What's the surprise?" she asked, kicking off shoes that did great things to her legs but not much else. "And where is it? Because if I have to go anywhere, you have to wait. My feet are killing me."

He pushed off the door and walked toward her, his hands in his pant pockets, the tails of his coat flaring behind him. "You'd like me to rub them, you say."

She arched a brow, trying not to drool at the fit of his clothes. His hips were so lean, his waist perfect. She pictured him naked, and bit back a groan. "Is that the surprise? A foot rub?"

He shrugged carelessly, the fabric hugging the muscles of his shoulders, tightening around his biceps. "It could be part of it."

"Is this a sex thing?" Because all he had to do was say the word. On the bed. On the floor. On her knees. Underneath. She didn't care.

"That could be part of it, too," he said as he reached her, as he stopped, doing nothing but staring into her eyes and making her sweat.

She crossed the room, flipped off the table lamp they'd left burning. Something in his gaze told her he wanted it dark. "You disappeared on me last night. I kept waiting for you. Where did you go?"

"You needed to sleep," he said, still not moving, still staring, still dressed. "I had things to take care of. With the chopper. With Hank."

She thought about what Jack had done in the warehouse, wondered if that was it. Wondered how he felt about killing a man who ruled an island. Wondered if it would give him nightmares, or if he'd rejoice. As she rejoiced.

"But I'm here now." His voice was low and raspy, his eyes flashing, his hands still in his pockets, his chest rising and falling as if he'd just run a race.

Funny. She couldn't breathe either. "We're here now. No Gabriel. No Joshua."

"Your son's a great kid," he said, nodding.

She smiled. "Not bad for a jungle boy."

"He's got a helluva jungle girl for a role model."

This time her smile was just for him, and maybe a bit for herself. "Will you think I'm crazy if I tell you that I miss it?"

He compressed his lips, shook his head, stayed where he was. "It's been your life for a lot of years. I'd think you were more crazy if you didn't."

Was he ever going to move? Did he know what he was doing to her? He did, didn't he?

He was doing it on purpose, making her sweat in a dress that cost a small fortune. "That doesn't mean I have to go back, you know."

He arched a brow, curled a lip, pulled his hands from his pockets. "Good, because I've had my fill of roughing it. I told you. Clean sheets and a bed."

"Does that mean you want to be where I am?" she asked, her fingers curling into the expensive fabric and marring it beyond all hope.

Finally. Oh, God, finally. He moved, coming close, sliding his hands around her waist and down to her bottom. He pulled her flush, standing there until his heart and her heart beat together.

"Of course I do," he said, his eyes swollen red with emotion. "I love you, Jillian Paige Endicott. And I plan to love you forever. I can do that best from where you are. But, no. My loving you is not the surprise."

He took her hand then and led her to the bathroom, undressing her once they were there.

She was naked when he dropped his tux on top of her gown, when he turned on the faucets, when he lifted her onto the vanity and loved her to the sound of water filling the room's claw-foot tub built for two.

Take a look at Karen Kelley's
CLOSE ENCOUNTERS OF
THE SEXY KIND.
Available now from Brava!

"Would you like something to eat?"

Eat? Mala had had two food capsules prior to leaving her planet, which was enough nutrition for one rotation, but she was curious about the food on Earth. Her grandmother had mentioned it was almost as good as sex. She just couldn't imagine that.

"Yes, food would be nice."

"Why don't you sit on the sofa and rest while I throw us something together." Mason picked up a black object. "Here's the remote. I have a satellite dish so you should be able to find something to entertain you while I rustle us up some food."

She nodded and took the remote, then watched him leave the room and go into another. The remote felt warm in her hand. A transferal of body heat? Tingles spread up and down her arm. The light above her head flickered.

She glanced up. Now, that was odd. But then, she *was* on Earth.

Her attention returned to the remote.

Very primitive. The history books on her planet had spoken about remote controls in the old days. You pointed it at the object it was programmed to work with so you wouldn't have to leave your seat.

She pointed it toward the door and pushed the power button. The door didn't open. She tried different objects around the room without success. Finally, she pointed toward a black box.

The screen immediately became a picture. Of course, television. She made herself comfortable on the lounging sofa and began clicking different channels. Everything interested her, but what she found most fascinating was a channel called Sensual Heat.

She tossed the remote to a small table and curled her feet under her, hugging the sofa pillow, her gaze glued to the screen. A naked man walked across the set, his tanned butt clenching and unclenching with every step he took. When he faced her, the man's erection stood tall, hypnotizing her. It was so large she couldn't take her gaze off it.

A naked woman appeared behind him. She slipped her arms around him, her hands splayed over his chest. Slowly, she began to move her hands over his body, inching them downward, ever closer.

Mala held her breath.

"I want you," the woman whispered. "I want to take you into my mouth, my tongue swirling around your hard cock."

The man groaned.

Mala leaned forward, biting her bottom lip as the man's hands snaked behind him and grabbed the woman's butt. In one swift movement, he turned around. "Damn, you make me hard with just your words."

"And I love when you talk dirty to me."

"So, you want me to tell you what I want to do to your body?"

The woman nodded.

He grinned, then began talking again. "I want to squeeze your breasts and rub my thumbs over your hard nipples." His actions followed his words. "You like that?"

"Yes!" She flung her head back, arching toward the man.

Mala leaned forward, her mouth dry, her body tingling with excitement. Yes! She wanted this, too!

"Do you like French bread, or white bread?" Mason asked, walking into the room.

She dragged her gaze from the television. Bred. That was what humans called copulating. Getting bred. Her nipples ached. "Yes, can we breed now?" She stood and began slipping her clothes off.

"No! That's not what I meant." He hurried forward and grabbed her dress as it slipped off one shoulder, quickly putting it back in place. Damn, what did Doc give her? This was one hell of a side effect.

"You don't want to copulate?" Her forehead wrinkled, causing her to wince and raise her hand to the bump on her head. "Do you find that I'm not to your liking?"

"Yes, I like you."

"But you do not wish to . . ." She bit her bottom lip as if searching for the right words. "To have sex?"

His hand rested lightly on her shoulder as he met her gaze. "Of course I'd like to . . . uh . . ." He marveled at how soft the fabric felt. His fingers brushed her skin, thinking it felt just as soft. What would she taste like? His gaze moved to her lips. Soft . . . full lips. Kissable.

He jerked his hand away from her shoulder. Anyone watching would think he'd been burned . . . and maybe he had because he certainly felt hot.

He cleared his throat, his gaze not able to meet those innocent, sensuous turquoise eyes. He felt like such a heel. He'd invited her to his home and all he could think about was having hot sex.

Don't miss the newest
release by Jill Shalvis,
SMART AND SEXY.
From Brava. In stores now.

Frustrated, uncharacteristically uptight, and . . . inexplicably aroused, Noah went around the Jeep for Bailey. Then he led her through the garage to the inside of the house.

He had no idea what it was about her, either that fierce pride in her eyes that said she'd rather not have needed his help, or the way he felt when she laid those eyes on him, or maybe it was more base than that, maybe it was simply her mouth-watering body.

He had no idea, but he tried to put it, and her, out of his head.

He'd stayed here before, many times, and was already familiar with the house. He cranked up the heat, all the while holding onto the soggy, still shivering woman.

The people who owned the house were incredibly wealthy but not showy. As usual, the place was clean, warm, and cozy. Just as he liked it. The living room opened into the kitchen, and on the counter was a basket filled with his favorite junk snacks: cookies, donuts, and chips. Maddie had had it stocked for him. "Hungry?"

Bailey looked at the offering and shook her head.

"Don't tell me. Health food nut."

"Good food never hurt anyone."

He, not nearly so picky, grabbed a large chocolate-chip cookie. While munching, he found her an apple, which she took with a wild shiver.

"Come on." He led her through the house and up to the master bedroom, where he would have pulled her into the bathroom, thinking a hot shower was what she needed, but she dug her heels into the carpet and shook her head more violently than the rest of her was shaking, which was really saying something.

"You need to get warm," he said.

"I'm fine."

Bullshit, she was fine. The car ride might have begun to warm her up but it hadn't fully done the job, and he needed to do something. Clearly she was pulling the shy card, but it was too late for that.

"N—no need for a shower," she said through chattering teeth.

"You have to get warm." He lifted his hands to his own shirt, which he unbuttoned.

Her eyes widened. "Um—what—"

"I don't know about you, but I'm just about done with being cold and wet."

"Yes, but—"

"Hurry."

Her gaze locked on his chest. "H-hurry to what?"

"*Strip.*"

Bailey could not have possibly heard him right. Strip? *Strip?* Was he insane? Suddenly being too scared to think and too frozen solid to imagine ever being warm again took a back seat to this new and entirely disconcerting situation.

She was alone in a house with a man she hardly knew, a big strong tough man who knew his way around trouble, who looked like sin on a stick, oh, and he'd *unbuttoned his shirt*.

Strip . . .

How was it even possible she wanted to do just that? She'd

seen men naked before, so she had no idea why the sight of Noah undoing his shirt, revealing a wedge of bare torso, made her mouth suddenly dry, but she wasn't sticking around to find out. "Noah—"

He took a step forward, and she took one back, which had the high mattress hitting her in the butt.

As if that had been his plan all along, his hands went to either side of her hips, resting on the thick bedding, his body close enough to share some of that heat he had radiating off of him, not to mention the sheer hard strength of him pressing against her.

Strip . . .

She wanted to, she really did, and it had nothing to do with impending hypothermia, and everything to do with how he made her feel when he looked at her, touched her.

Kissed her.

God. She was really losing it here, as surely as the room was beginning to warm from the hot air coming out of the heater vents, enclosing them in an intimacy she wasn't sure she could face. He couldn't really want her, could he? Not after what she'd done, dragging him here.

Putting his life in danger.

That last thought made her breath catch, made her hug herself and close her eyes, until he lifted her chin. He'd stepped close, close enough that his broad shoulders blocked out the light. "Just want to warm you up, Bailey."

She *was* cold, *beyond* cold, and shaking so hard she could feel her brain cells rattling together.

But still, she could think.

And what she thought was that things were worse than ever. She hadn't found the money. One resort down, two more to check. And now that Noah had helped her lose the men on her tail, she should go immediately. That meant going back out there . . .

Closing her eyes again, she weaved in exhaustion, then felt

his hands on her arms again. "Hey," he said, bending a little to peer into her face. "Hey, it's going to be okay."

"Really? How?" She didn't pull away, she no longer had the energy, the cold had sapped it right out of her. "I'm sorry," she whispered. "I have to go. I need to call a cab, or—"

"No. Hell, no." With that he dropped his shirt to the floor and pulled her into the heat of his body. "No one's going anywhere, not tonight."

And now a peek at
SATISFACTION GUARANTEED
by Lucy Monroe.
Coming next month from Brava!

B eth was shaking with nerves by the time that Ethan buzzed her condo that night.

She'd told herself over and over again that this was not a real date. It was an opportunity to solidify their cover. Right. And the fact that they would be sitting across an intimate table for two should not be sending her libido into overdrive. She'd read somewhere that women were at the sexual peak in their thirties. Well, she was only twenty-nine and she'd been peaking for Ethan for almost two years.

Which meant it wasn't some kind of hormonal joke her body was playing on her. She wanted the man. So much that she'd stopped calling herself depraved and learned to deal with the urges. Only now she was faced with more temptation than she'd ever had where he was concerned. She didn't know if she could deal with that.

Darn him anyway for being the one man she was sure would not only not balk at her sexual fantasies, but who would know what to do with them.

She bit her lip as she took a final look in her full-length mirror. She had not morphed into a cover model for *Vogue* in the last ten seconds, more the pity. Because while she was sure Ethan would understand her sexual fantasies, she was equally certain he would have no interest in sharing them. She was not his type.

At five-foot-six, she was at least three inches too short, a cup size too small in the curves department and several lovers shy of the experience a man like him was no doubt used to.

None of that had stopped her from trying on six different outfits, doing her makeup three times, and trying her hair four different ways before settling for a sloppy topknot with tendrils framing her face that went well with the simple black dress she'd settled on. It left a good portion of her legs and back bare . . . all in the effort to look as sexy as she could for him. For this non-date. Sheesh.

She needed to get a life.

The problem was that she didn't want a life . . . she wanted *him*. Every sexy, tantalizing, irresistible inch of his six-foot-three frame.

The buzzer rang again and she jumped, grimacing. Show-time.

She rushed to release the entrance lock for downstairs. Ethan was knocking on her door less than a minute later.

She opened it, keeping the kittens back with one wary foot. "Hi."

"Hi, Sunshine. Is there a reason you're blocking the door?"

"The kittens." She scooted back, keeping the cats away from the opening as she widened it to let him in. "Come on in and I'll get my jacket."

Ethan moved swiftly, grabbing Beethoven as the black and white kitten tried to make a break for the hall and shutting the door immediately upon stepping inside her apartment.

"Thanks. They want to go exploring, but with my luck they'd end up at the manager's apartment. She's allergic to feline fur and was very dubious about letting me get the cats."

Ethan grinned. "I can imagine." He whistled as he looked around. "Nice place. Exotic."

That's what she'd been going for. She'd decorated with

Byzantine colors and rich textures like silks and velvets as well as faux fur throws on her sofa and chaise lounge. It fit her, but usually surprised people who did not know her well. Even some who did.

Ethan didn't looked surprised, only intrigued.

She grabbed her vintage velvet dress coat from the back of the chair where she'd left it in preparation. "I'm ready to go, if you are."

"Dinner's not for another hour." He took the coat and laid it back over the chair.

Then he shrugged off his own leather jacket and put it on top of hers. And she let him. Without a protest. Weird. This man brought out more than one unexpected reaction in her. Even odder . . . she just stood there staring at him and trying really hard to remember—*this was not a real date.*

But his dark sweater clung to his muscular chest in a mouthwatering manner. He looked so hot . . . in every way.

He cocked his brow at her and her stomach dipped. "Um . . . if not dinner yet, then what?"

"I thought we could have a drink and talk a while before we go." He looked around her living room again. "I want a chance to soak in who you are away from the office so I can relate to that person in front of Preston."

It sounded reasonable, but Ethan Crane was the last person she wanted to invite into her life on a more personal basis.